"Nobody's watching," she said.

"Then no one will see if I do this."

He spun her around in his arms and pulled her against him. Her arms stretched to wrap around his huge torso. She loved the way she fit against him; the way he held her close felt so good. So right.

"We shouldn't be doing this," she murmured. "I'm in charge of the safe house. I should be setting an example."

His lips silenced her. With his kiss, he exploded the apprehension that had been building inside her. Her defensive wall of propriety crumbled to dust. With a soft moan, she gave herself completely to this fierce, demanding passion.

When he separated from her, she gasped. Her heartbeat throbbed like a big bass drum. It took a big man to sweep her off her feet. Paul was that man.

CASSIE MILES

MURDER ON THE MOUNTAIN

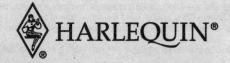

TORONTO • NEW YORK • LONDON
AMSTERDAM • PARIS • SYDNEY • HAMBURG
STOCKHOLM • ATHENS • TOKYO • MILAN • MADRID
PRAGUE • WARSAW • BUDAPEST • AUCKLAND

To Kayla and Landon.
And, as always, to Rick.

ISBN 0-373-88684-5

MURDER ON THE MOUNTAIN

ABOUT THE AUTHOR

For Cassie Miles, the best part about writing a story set in Eagle County near the Vail ski area is the ready-made excuse to head into the mountains for research. Though the winter snows are great for skiing, her favorite season is fall when the aspens turn gold.

The rest of the time, Cassie lives in Denver where she takes urban hikes around Cheesman Park, reads a ton and critiques often. Her current plans include a Vespa and a road trip, despite eye-rolling objections from her adult children.

Books by Cassie Miles

CAST OF CHARACTERS

Julia Last—The FBI Special Agent in charge of the safe house is torn between protecting her secrecy and solving a murder.

Paul Hemmings—The Eagle County deputy sheriff knows something is wrong at the safe house and fears for Julia.

Jennifer and Lily Hemmings—Paul's daughters, aged seven and nine, want to be ice skating princesses though their father prefers hockey.

John Maser—Also known as Johnny Maserati, he dies in a car wreck.

Harrison Naylor—The four-star marine general dies in uniform in his locked bedroom, an apparent suicide.

Marcus Ashbrook—The senator from Wyoming hopes to use the Homeland Security exercise at the safe house to further his career.

Gil Bradley—The mysterious and muscular CIA agent might have a history as an assassin.

RJ Katz—The FBI Special Agent is an expert in accounting scams.

David Dillard—The FBI computer specialist arranges the simulation exercise for Homeland Security.

Garret Dillard—David's brother is a hero in the marines.

Roger Flannery—The rookie FBI Special Agent working at the safe house has developed a talent for cooking.

Chapter One

Deputy Paul Hemmings stood at the edge of the cliff looking down. Far below, a midsized sedan was wedged upside down against a tall pine. Morning sunlight reflected dully on the muddy undercarriage and tires. A bad accident. Not uncommon on these mountain roads. Especially at this time of year, early December.

Yet there were no skid marks. The pavement was dry. Ice wasn't a hazard. Why, Paul wondered, had this vehicle gone off the road?

The woman who had flagged him down asked, "Can I leave now?"

"I've put through a call for assistance, ma'am. The rescue team should be here soon."

"But I'm supposed to meet my husband at Vail Village in fifteen minutes."

"Sorry. You have to stay so you can give a report to the investigating officers."

"There's really nothing to tell," she said. "I pulled onto the shoulder to take a picture of that frozen waterfall. I'm an amateur photographer, and it's a beautiful morning and—"

"Stop." Paul held up a hand. "I can't take your statement. I'm off duty."

He glanced at his Ford Explorer SUV. The faces of his two young daughters, Jennifer and Lily, pressed up against the windows. They'd been on their way to the ice-skating rink for their lesson when this witness signaled him to stop. His girls were going to be plenty ticked off about arriving late to Saturday practice.

And so was this witness who stabbed at the buttons on her cell phone. "I can't even call my husband. I've got no signal."

"Accidents are inconvenient," he said. "Especially for the person driving."

Had that person survived?

Highly unlikely. However, if the driver had survived, it was Paul's duty to offer assistance until the rescue team arrived. He stepped over the ridge of dirty snow that marked the shoulder of the two-lane mountain road.

The descent was rocky and steep, but this was the sunny side of the valley and much of the snow had melted. So far, this had been a mild winter. Too mild. The workers at the ski resorts were praying for a blizzard.

He sidestepped down the slope. Though he was a big man—over six feet four and weighing more than was good for his cholesterol—Paul moved with surefooted balance. He'd been born and raised in these mountains; climbing was in his DNA.

As he approached the overturned car, he noted that the earth was torn up from the car's plummet, but there were no footprints. None leading away from the wreck. None leading toward it.

At the driver's side, he hunkered down. Though the car rested on the roof, the interior hadn't been crushed too badly. The driver's-side window was broken out. There was a man inside. And blood. A lot of blood.

"Sir?" Paul reached inside the car to touch the shoulder of this man. Half of his forehead was a bloody pulp. His complexion had the waxen sheen of a death mask. His lips were blue. He couldn't still be alive. If his injuries from the accident hadn't killed him, exposure to the night cold would have finished him off.

Yet, he moved. His eyelids twitched. He whispered one word. "Murder."

I'M GOING TO MURDER this guy. FBI Special Agent Julia Last glared daggers into the broad shoulders of the distinguished, silver-haired man who had started making demands the minute he walked through the door.

After eleven years with the FBI, she didn't appreciate being treated like a housemaid. Julia was the agent in charge here. The operation of this two-story, nine-bedroom FBI safehouse in Eagle County, Colorado was her responsibility, and she'd managed it well enough to receive several commendations. Dozens of protected witnesses had come under her care. She'd also provided a haven for agents and officers who had been injured in the line of duty and needed recuperation time. Never once, during her two-year tenure at the safehouse, had security been breached.

Her latest guest—the silver-haired jerk—regarded his second-floor bedroom with blatant disdain, then turned to face her. "I'll take my first cup of coffee at six in the morning. Low-fat milk and one teaspoon of sugar. Not a sugar substitute. Delivered to my room along with *The Wall Street Journal*."

"We don't provide room service," Julia said through gritted teeth. "All meals are family-style in the dining room."

"My coffee at six," he repeated. "And the *Journal*."

"You might have noticed that this is a rather remote location." The safehouse was four miles down a graded gravel road through a heavily forested wilderness area. "Newspaper deliveries are much later than six."

He glanced around the clean but relatively plain bedroom. "Where's the television?"

"We have a TV downstairs."

"Unacceptable. How am I supposed to keep up on the news if I can't watch CNN?" He tapped his chest. "I need to stay abreast of developments. Do you know who I am?"

"Yes, sir." Senator Marcus Ashbrook from Wyoming had been mentioned as a possible candidate for president. Needless to say, if Julia had resided in that state, he wouldn't get her vote.

"I'll need a television in my room." He flashed his photogenic smile and held out a five-dollar bill. "That will be all."

He was offering her a tip? This was too much. Julia snatched the bill from his hand and slammed it down on the knotty pine dresser. "I'm not a concierge, sir. And this is not a hotel."

"You're supposed to make me comfortable."

"It's my job to keep you safe," she corrected him. "This FBI safehouse might look like a rustic mountain lodge, but we're equipped with state-of-the-art security. While you're here, I will expect you to abide by our rules and to accept our restrictions."

"Will you now?" He looked surprised; the senator wasn't accustomed to having underlings tell him what to do.

"If it's necessary for you to leave the premises, I must be notified. No guests permitted. Three meals a day are served in the dining room. And, of course, tell no one that this is a safehouse."

"Why not?"

Could he really be that stupid? She didn't think so. Senator Marcus Ashbrook hadn't risen through the ranks of national politics by being a moron. "The whole purpose of a safehouse is to provide a covert location to keep the 'guests' safe. Security depends on keeping our mission secret from the bad guys."

"Good answer." Again, the photogenic smile.

She eyed him suspiciously. "Were you testing me, Senator?"

"I was indeed. I've heard that you're good at your job, Agent Last."

She dredged up an insincere smile of her own. "Thank you, sir. I prefer to be called Julia."

"Of course you do."

She turned on her heel and left his bedroom. This was going to be a long, strenuous, annoying week. The only "guests" at the safehouse were five high-ranking individuals who were involved with a Homeland Security project. In addition to the senator, there was a four-star Marine general, a former Navy SEAL who was now CIA and two senior FBI agents.

Though Julia didn't know the precise agenda for this group, she was certain that she and her live-in staff of two agents were going to have their hands full. Managing all these egos wouldn't be easy.

"Excuse me, Julia."

Now what? She turned and saw Gil Bradley, the CIA agent, standing in the center of the hallway. She could have sworn that the door to his room was closed, and she hadn't heard it open. Nor did she register the sound of his footsteps on the creaky hardwood floor. He'd just appeared. Like the spook that he was.

Gil Bradley was obviously the muscle in this group. His massive shoulders and well-developed arms suggested that he was capable of bench-pressing a giant redwood. But he was still able to move silently. Spooky, indeed. "What can I do for you, Gil?"

"I'm allergic to shellfish." His rasping voice made it sound like he was imparting a state secret.

"Thanks for telling me. I don't think we have shrimp on the menu for this week." Apparently, he was *not* allergic to dirt. His jeans were streaked with mud. "Have you been out hiking?"

"I run five miles every day. Rain, shine or snow."

"Admirable."

His gaze rested on her full hips. "You should come with me. Lean and mean, Julia. Lean and mean."

He zipped back into his room. The door closed with an audible click before she had a chance to tell him that she might not look like the Barbie version of GI Jane but would gladly match her physical conditioning and stamina against anyone. Even him.

At the foot of the staircase, she stalked through the great room, past the long oak dining table and into the kitchen. Roger Flannery, a young agent who had been at the safehouse for three months and discovered a talent for cooking, stood at the counter, chopping with the speed and aplomb of a sushi chef.

She should have been pleased with Roger's dedication to providing a semigourmet dinner every night, but Julia was still cranky after her encounters with Senator Ashbrook and Gil Bradley. When she was in this kind of mood, it was better not to stop and chitchat. She made a beeline through the kitchen toward the back door.

"Hey, Julia," Roger said.

She growled a response and kept walking.

If Roger had any self-preservation instinct at all, he wouldn't say another word.

"Wait a sec," he said. "I could use some help with dinner."

She muttered a negative, but that wasn't sufficient for peppy Roger-Dodger. "What's eating you?" he asked. "You look like a grizzly that swallowed a wasp nest."

Slowly, she turned. "A grizzly?"

Roger chuckled. "Yeah."

"Is that a reference to my hair?" Her long brown hair was notoriously curly and wild even when pulled back in a ponytail.

"N-n-no."

"Or maybe you were thinking of my size when you said I look like a grizzly." Nearly six feet tall in her hiking boots, she had a broad-shouldered, muscular frame that made comparisons to a bear somewhat plausible. "Gil thinks I should step up my exercise program."

"You look g-great," Roger said, frantically backpedaling as his gaze darted, taking in the details of her jeans, white turtleneck and plaid wool shirt. "Nice outfit."

"Can't say the same for you." He'd stripped down to a black T-shirt revealing his shoulder holster. Hadn't she just lectured the senator about keeping the true purpose of the safehouse a secret? "Put a shirt on. Cover that weapon."

"But it's hot in here."

"Do it." She shoved open the door that led onto a spacious cedar deck at the rear of the safehouse.

The December air cooled her face as she walked across the deck to the railing. The sight of clear blue skies above a wide valley bordered by forest gave her a momentary surge of pleasure. She loved the rugged majesty of the Colorado mountains, especially at this time of year when swathes of drifted snow gleamed pearly white in the afternoon sunlight. Though the ski areas were open and had a solid snow base, much of the snowfall near the safehouse had already melted into the thirsty earth.

In the midst of all this grandeur, did she still feel annoyance at the way she'd been treated by the senator? Or at the thinly veiled criticism from Gil? Was she still mad? Yes, most definitely. And she needed to lose this attitude before confronting the Homeland Security hotshots over dinner.

Unfortunately, there wasn't time to run down to the barn, saddle up one of the horses and ride. The next best thing for blowing off steam was chopping wood.

She tromped heavily down the stairs and along a path to a storage shed where several cords of logs were neatly stacked and waiting along with work gloves and a well-honed ax. After pulling on her stiff leather gloves, she carried a couple of fat logs to the outdoor chopping block where she would split them into an appropriate size for the fireplace in the great room.

With the log positioned on the block, she drew back and swung with all her strength. The ax head made contact and the wood split. A satisfying jolt went through her body. Again and again, she attacked the logs. This was a better workout than a heavy punching bag. She imagined the senator's face before the ax descended in a fierce and graceful arc. *Take that, you jerk.*

Julia caught a glimpse of movement in her peripheral vision and turned. There was a man watching her with his arms folded across his chest. He wore the brown uniform jacket for the Eagle County Sheriff's Department.

"I didn't want to interrupt." He came closer and held out his hand. "I'm Deputy Paul Hemmings."

"Julia Last."

Their gloved hands met. His grip was strong, and she appreciated that he didn't hold back because she was a woman. Though she'd seen the deputy in town when she shopped for supplies, Julia hadn't appreciated those broad shoulders and barrel chest until this moment. Paul Hemmings was a very tall, very impressive man.

Despite his extra-large dimensions, he wasn't hulking or threatening. He had an easygoing smile. His strong white teeth contrasted his tanned complexion. Sunlight glistened in his thick black hair. She wished he'd take off his sunglasses so she could see the color of his eyes. "What brings you here, Deputy?"

"I've been wanting to pay a visit," he said. "A friend of mine, Mac Granger, stayed here a couple of months ago. He liked the place."

"I remember Mac." He'd been involved in a sting operation that turned ugly. "Got himself into a bit of trouble."

"That's putting it mildly." He bent and picked up the chunks of wood she'd split. "I'll help you carry this load inside."

Which was a subtly clever way of getting an inside peek at the safehouse. She didn't for one minute believe that Deputy Paul Hemmings had popped in for a casual howdy.

Julia rested her hand on the ax handle. "Why don't you tell me the real reason you stopped by?"

"You like to get right to the point."

"I do," she said. "So?"

"There was a car accident last night. The driver went off the road, flipped his rental car. He was DOA at the hospital."

"Sorry to hear that."

"He had a note in his wallet with the phone number for your lodge written on it."

Her protective instincts were immediately aroused. Though the safehouse had a regular phone listing, the message was always the same: Sorry, we're booked. There were never outside guests. Feigning disinterest, she said, "Maybe he was looking for a place to stay."

"Or he might have wanted to contact one of your guests. The man who died was from Washington, D.C."

As were all the people involved in the Homeland Security project. Julia didn't like where this conversation was headed. "I hate to have you bothering my guests."

"I promise to be quick, Julia. Is it okay if I call you Julia?"

"If I can call you Paul."

"You bet." He glanced down at the logs in his arms. "Where do you want these?"

"We have enough wood inside. Just bring them into the storage shed."

Inside the dimly lit shed, she watched as Paul methodically placed the logs in a neat stack. Though he seemed like someone who could be trusted with a secret, she didn't want *anybody* to know the true purpose of the safehouse. Not even the local law enforcement. If one person knew, then another would and another. Then word would leak. Security would be compromised.

As Paul finished with the woodpile, he took off his sunglasses and turned to her. His eyes were a beautiful chocolate-brown. When she gazed into their depths, Julia felt something inside her begin to melt. For one fleeting second, she imagined what it would be like to be held by those big, strong arms. The broad expanse of his chest would provide ample room for her to snuggle. His flesh would be warm. His lips would be gentle.

She blinked, erasing these inappropriate

thoughts. Where did that little burst of wild-eyed lust come from? It had been a long time since she'd been with a man, mostly because her responsibilities at the safehouse made dating difficult. But that was her choice. Her career. And the lack of a meaningful relationship didn't bother her.

But maybe it did. Maybe that was the real reason why her emotions were all over the place. Maybe she needed more than chopping wood to control her anger. Maybe she needed to get laid.

"What's wrong?" Paul asked.

"Nothing," she said quickly.

"I should talk to your guests now."

When he gave her a broad smile, his cheeks dimpled. He was just too sexy for words. Her repressed imagination again caught fire. She wanted to kiss those dimples, to taste his mouth.

He took a step toward her.

Julia's breath quickened.

She heard, very clearly, a gunshot.

Chapter Two

Paul charged through the door of the shed with his gun drawn. "Julia, stay back."

"No way."

Another gunshot. Paul looked up.

Standing on the cedar deck behind the lodge was an older man, bald with a neatly trimmed fringe of graying hair around his ears. His posture was ramrod straight. He stood with legs apart and one hand behind his back. With the other hand, he aimed a chrome automatic handgun into a nearby stand of trees. What the hell did he think he was doing?

"Freeze." Paul sighted down the barrel of his gun. "Police."

The bald man looked down his nose. "Nothing to worry about, young man."

Paul thought otherwise. Without lowering his gun, he climbed the staircase to the deck. "Drop your weapon."

"You're overreacting." He squatted and carefully placed his gun on the deck floor. "I was just taking target practice, shooting at a rabbit."

"Hunting season is over." Paul scooped up the weapon. A Colt Double Eagle. A nice piece. And well cared for.

Julia stepped onto the deck behind him. "Deputy Paul Hemmings, I'd like to introduce General Harrison Naylor."

The general's squint and his square jaw seemed familiar. His formal bearing gave Paul the feeling that he was supposed to snap to attention and salute. But he had guns in both hands, so he merely nodded. "Army?"

"Marines," the general said.

Which still didn't give him the right to take potshots off the deck. "I'm sure you don't need a lecture on gun safety, General. In future, if you want to take target practice, choose a less populated location."

"Away from the barn," Julia added. "We have several horses, and they're not accustomed to gunfire."

Reluctantly, Paul returned the Colt Double Eagle. The general took a white handkerchief from his pocket and wiped the moisture from the gleaming silver gun. Though dressed in a casual cardigan, the man was impeccable. His trousers held a razor crease, and his shirt was buttoned all the way up to the collar.

Paul cleared his throat. "I'm here because of a car accident. The driver was from Washington, D.C., and I have reason to believe he was looking for someone staying here."

"I'm stationed in D.C.," the general said.

"The driver's name was John Maser."

The general paused for a moment. His lips moved as he silently repeated the name several times. "That's Maser as in Maserati?"

"Yes, sir."

"It's hard to remember all of the men I've had under my command. You said there was a car accident. What happened to Maserati?"

"He was killed."

"A shame." The general shook his head. "Can't say that I know the gentleman."

Paul was dead certain that he'd seen the general before. "Do you come to this area often? Maybe for skiing?"

"This is my first time. I usually ski in Utah."

"General Naylor, have we met?"

"I don't believe so."

"You might have seen the general on television," Julia said. "He does a lot of expert commentary."

"You can't believe everything you see on TV," the general said. "Nothing they've said about me is the truth. Not one damned thing."

He executed a sharp turn and marched through the door into the lodge.

Paul exchanged glances with Julia, who seemed as puzzled by the general's statement as he was. "Interesting guest."

"Very," she said.

"How many other people are staying here?"

"Four. And I have two full-time guys who help me run the place."

Since it was obvious that she didn't want to invite him inside, Paul took the initiative. He held open the storm door. "After you."

As she sauntered past him, her curly ponytail came so close that he could smell the fresh scent of her shampoo. There was no other perfume on Julia. She didn't seem like the type to fuss with girlie things. And yet, she was all woman.

When he'd seen her chopping wood behind the resort, Paul's heart had pounded harder than thunder across the valley. He'd been stunned, unable to do anything more than stand and stare as this Amazon raised the ax over her head and swung down with force. She'd been breathing hard from her exertions. Inside her white turtleneck, her full breasts heaved. Damn, but she had a fine figure. An hourglass shape.

She reminded him of the early settlers in these mountains—women who were strong, resourceful and brave. And beautiful. Her complexion flushed with abundant health. Her eyes were blue—the color of a winter sky after a snowfall had washed the heavens clean.

Unfortunately, it seemed that she didn't particularly want him around. Not that she was rude. Just standoffish. He wondered if one of the men who helped her run the lodge was her boyfriend.

In the kitchen, she introduced him to a young man who was doing the cooking for dinner. Though Paul was pleased to see that their relationship fell into the category of boss and employee, there was something disturbing about this guy. Young Roger

Flannery had the bulge of a shoulder holster under his flannel shirt. Not illegal. But worrying.

A small, sleek woman entered the kitchen, and Julia introduced her. "Another of our guests. This is RJ Katz."

She looked like a cat with a button nose, a tiny mouth and wide, suspicious eyes. As Paul shook her thin hand, he asked, "Where are you from?"

"I travel a lot."

That was an evasive answer if he'd ever heard one. "Business or pleasure?"

"Both."

Just like a cat. Snooty, cool and independent. When RJ Katz sidled toward the fridge, he half expected to see her take out a bowl of cream and lap it up with her tongue.

If the car crash of John Maser turned out to be something more than an accident, Paul would put RJ at the head of his suspect list. "I need to see your driver's license, Ms. Katz."

"It's in my purse. In my room." She popped the tab on a cola and took a sip. "What's this about?"

Paul explained about the car accident and the victim from Washington, D.C. He watched for her reaction when he mentioned the name John Maser.

She was unruffled. "Don't know him."

"I'd still like to see your license."

"I suppose you're wondering if I live near D.C. Well, I do. My address is Alexandria, Virginia. But I assure you, Deputy, I don't know your victim."

There was a lot more he wanted to ask, but Paul had promised Julia that he wouldn't harass her guests. "Enjoy your stay."

Before they left the kitchen, Julia directed a question toward RJ Katz. "Do you know if David is in his room?"

"He's in the basement," she said, "playing with his precious computer."

"I'd appreciate if you asked him to come up here and speak with the deputy. So we don't have to go downstairs."

An unspoken communication passed between the two women, but Paul couldn't guess why. He was beginning to think that something strange was going on at this rustic little resort. There was the cook with a shoulder holster. And the feline Ms. Katz who seemed determined to hide her identity. And, of course, a general who gunned down jackrabbits from the porch.

When Paul first arrived, he had noticed three satellite dishes that might be for extra-fine television reception or for some other kind of communication. Clearly, he needed more information about Julia and the lodge.

She led him through the dining room to the front area where a cheery fire burned in the moss rock fireplace. Comfortable was the first word that popped into his head. The sturdy leather sofas and chairs looked big enough to sink into and relax. "Nice," he said. "I could see myself sitting in that big chair on a Sunday afternoon watching the football game."

"How about those Broncos?"

"Are you a fan?"

"Actually, I prefer hockey."

"Me, too."

Damn, he liked this woman. He really hoped there was nothing sinister going on here.

She stepped in front of him and looked him directly in the eye. "I want to level with you, Paul."

"Go ahead."

"All five of my guests are from the Washington, D.C., area. They're here for a retreat and meetings."

The presence of the high-profile general who appeared on talk shows suggested a topic for those meetings. "Something political."

"I really shouldn't say."

"What you're telling me is that any one of your guests might be acquainted with the man who was killed."

"Yes," she said.

Paul was sure that if they knew anything about the death of John Maser, these people wouldn't be forthcoming with information. More in-depth questioning and investigation was necessary. He needed to verify their alibis and arrival times.

On the other hand, he might be bothering these people for no reason at all. John Maser might have died as a result of careless driving. Nothing more.

After the autopsy, Paul would have a better indication of foul play. Right now, his only evidence was the whispered word of the dying man who might have been out of his head. *Murder.*

"I have a thought," Julia said. "It's almost time for dinner, and everybody will be gathered in one place. You can talk to all of them at the same time."

Not a great idea from the aspect of police procedure. One-on-one questioning was a more effective tool. But this wasn't really an investigation. Not yet anyway. "Fine with me."

This time Julia held the front door open for him. "After you."

He stepped onto the covered porch that stretched all the way across the front of the lodge. From this vantage point, there was a clear view of the gravel drive leading up to the lodge and the vehicles that were parked in the front, including a Hummer that probably belonged to the general.

He sat in one of the rocking chairs, and Julia climbed onto the porch swing. She didn't speak right away, but the silence wasn't uncomfortable. He liked her self-assurance—a maturity that didn't require the constant chatter that filled his house when his girls got revved. "How do you feel about kids, Julia?"

"Love them." Her face lit up. "My one regret about living here is that I don't get to spend more time with my niece and nephew back in Wisconsin. They're practically teenagers now."

"I have two daughters. Seven and nine."

"They must keep your wife busy."

"Not so you'd notice. My ex-wife left a long time ago. I guess we didn't have much in common." *Not like you and me,* he wanted to add.

"Raising two little girls on your own must be hard."

The way she looked at him, giving him her full attention, made Paul feel like spilling his guts. He wanted to tell her about how frustrated he got when the girls burst into tears for no reason he could understand. Or how confused he was when they changed clothes five times before walking out the door. He wanted to tell Julia about the feeling of sheer happiness when one of the girls hopped onto his lap and told him he was the best daddy in the world.

Julia's smile encouraged him, and he wanted to tell her everything, wanted to hear her laugh. Or maybe he just wanted to sit here on the porch and watch as the last rays of sunset tangled in her thick, curly hair. His gaze stuck on her lips, and his thoughts turned toward kisses. Caresses. Making love in the afternoon.

"What are their names?" she asked.

"Who?"

"Your kids."

"Jennifer and Lily." His thoughts had moved far beyond the kids. "Maybe sometime when you're not busy, you'd go out to dinner with me."

Those beautiful lips pinched, and he was pretty sure she was going to tell him to take a hike. Instead, she said, "Next week?"

"It's a date."

He leaned back in the rocking chair and grinned. A date with Julia. Damn, this was going to be good.

A glint of sunlight caught his eye. When he looked toward the roof of the covered porch, he spotted the camouflaged lens of a surveillance camera. Again, he wondered what was really going on here.

SHE SHOULDN'T HAVE agreed to go out with him. Alone in the kitchen, Julia loaded the last of the dinner dishes into the washer. And she thought about her date with Paul Hemmings. The pros and the cons. Her mind seesawed.

A chirpy little voice whispered in one ear, "Go on the date. Paul's a good-looking man. Have some fun for a change."

In the other ear was a stern professional tone. "Paul is too smart. He'll figure out that this is a safehouse. Your career will be ruined."

She couldn't take that chance. Julia had worked too hard to get to this level. Her FBI career was her whole life.

"That's pathetic," said the chirpy voice that sounded a little bit like her mother. "You're thirty-two years old. Don't you want to have a family? Children of your own?"

Paul already had a family. Two girls.

Julia shook her head. She was getting way ahead of herself. He hadn't asked her to marry him, after all. It was only a date.

David Dillard, the FBI computer specialist, sauntered into the kitchen. "Any coffee left? I'm going to be up late."

"I was just about to make a fresh pot." Julia and the other two agents at the safehouse would be staying up all night in shifts to monitor the surveillance cameras that were posted in the hallways and outside. To stay alert, caffeine was a necessary evil.

David pushed his glasses up on the bridge of his nose and took a seat at the kitchen table. Of all the Homeland Security specialists who were staying here, she liked David best. He was an average looking guy—

pleasant and unassuming. "This is a excellent facility," he said.

"You've hardly been outside."

"I was talking about the lower level."

"The basement? But it's all white and sterile."

"For a computer geek like me, that's heaven."

To each his own. Julia spent as little time as possible in the basement where the charming, rustic lodge transformed into a high-tech operation with computers, communication devices and surveillance monitors. Most of the meetings for the Homeland Security group would take place in a bland windowless room on the lower level.

"I thought you brought your own computer with you," Julia said. "And that collapsible screen thing."

"Tools of the trade." He gave her a weary grin. "I'm setting up a series of simulations over the next several days."

"Simulating what?"

"Our project is to establish a protocol for first response teams handling crisis situations. We want to set up five-person teams of experts who can step in and run things in the chaos following a disaster. They would be the ultimate authority."

Thus far, no one else had bothered to explain the purpose of this meeting. Though Julia had been curious, she was accustomed to FBI people who played it close to the vest. Apparently, David didn't have reservations about talking.

"Isn't there already a chain of command?" she asked as she ground the fresh beans for coffee.

"Too many commanders," he said. "That's the problem. The people who are here represent various authorities. The senator to handle political issues. The general for military. RJ is a financial specialist. I'm a communications person. And, of course, there's Gil representing the CIA."

"What's Gil's specialty?"

David shrugged. "He looks like an assassin to me."

A charming thought. But she suspected David was correct. The sneaky but musclebound Gil Bradley looked like the kind of guy who could be dropped behind enemy lines to take out the opposition.

"What kind of crisis would you deal with?" she asked.

"There's the obvious big stuff, like a terrorist bombing. I have that simulation set up for the last day, and it's got really amazing effects. But there are smaller issues. Attacks on a high-profile target, like the Golden Gate bridge. A siege at a survivalist compound. Hostage-taking."

Julia shuddered as she watched the coffee slowly drip through the filter into the pot. "That's the worst," she said. "Hostages."

When it came to her own personal safety, she was fearless. But a threat to someone she loved? To her mother and father? She remembered the horror and pain she'd felt when she learned of her older brother's death three years ago. He'd been a Marine. In harm's way.

"Setting up an official response team is an exciting project," David said. "On paper, it looks like a snap. The problems come in dealing with all these authoritative personalities. Like the general, for example. His plan is always the same—Send in the Marines."

"Like my brother," she said. "He was a Marine."

"No kidding," David said. "Mine, too."

"So you know that the Marines are well trained for crisis."

"If it's a military crisis, yes. But there's so much more to consider. RJ with her financial expertise brings a whole different perspective."

The aroma of brewing coffee filled the kitchen. "What do finances have to do with homeland security?"

"If you close down the money spigot, the terrorists are left high and dry."

The coffee was done, and she poured a mug for David. "Thanks for the explanation. It's nice to have some idea about what's going on."

"Simulations are only half of what we're doing. There's also going to be team-building stuff."

"So you'll all learn to like one another?"

"That's too much to hope for," he said with a wry grin. "We'll be doing well if we don't all kill one another by the end of the week."

He grabbed his coffee and disappeared into the lower level. Julia probably should have followed him. There were daily reports she needed to file, but they weren't due until morning and that computer work would give her something to do while watching the monitors.

In spite of the coffee, it was nine o'clock when she fell into bed exhausted. Her alarm was set for three, when she was scheduled to take her shift at the monitors.

When she closed her eyes, her thoughts immediately flashed on Paul Hemmings. In her mind, she saw his chocolate eyes and the deep dimples in his cheeks. And his body. His large muscular body.

Her arms wrapped tightly around her pillow, and she imagined what it would be like to embrace him. It would take at least three pillows for that simulation.

It wasn't safe to feel this way. If only he hadn't asked her out, she could dream about Paul without regret. But he wanted to see her again, and that might be her undoing.

THE NEXT MORNING, everyone was up early except for the general, which seemed odd for a military man who ought to be accustomed to morning exercises. Julia was a bit worried when she stood outside the locked door of the general's bedroom and knocked. "Sir? Are you awake?"

She pressed her ear against the door and listened. There was no sound from inside.

Though she hated to disturb his privacy,

Julia unlocked the door to the general's bedroom.

He was flat on his bed, dressed in his uniform with medals and ribbons arrayed across his chest. In his right hand was his Colt Double Eagle handgun. General Harrison Naylor had shot himself in the head.

Chapter Three

Early Sunday morning, Paul had the girls loaded in the Explorer and on their way to another practice session at the ice-skating rink near Vail. The kids had a performance tonight, and their coach wanted to use every possible minute on the ice for practice.

When they passed the spot on the highway where they had been flagged down yesterday, both girls stared in silence through the car windows. Though Paul had gotten them away from the scene of the accident before the emergency rescue team went into action, they knew what had happened. Word spread fast in their community. Though they were close to Vail, they were separate. Redding was the kind of town where everybody knew everything.

"Daddy?" Jennifer, his nine-year-old,

sounded subdued. "That man in the crashed-up car died, didn't he?"

Like every parent, he wished to shield his kids from death and tragedy. There was no easy way to talk about these things. "Yes, Jennifer. The man died."

"But you tried to rescue him."

"I tried, but I was too late. It was a very bad accident."

From the back seat, seven-year-old Lily piped up, "It's okay, Daddy. I love you."

"Me, too." Jennifer reached over and patted his arm.

"I love you back." Apparently, they'd decided that he needed comforting, and he appreciated their effort. His daughters weren't always so sweet and sensitive. These two adorable, black-haired girls with porcelain complexions could be hell on wheels. "Have I ever mentioned that you kids are pretty amazing?"

"Yes," Lily said firmly. "I'm very pretty."

Jennifer groaned. "That's not what he meant, dorkface."

"Is too."

"Is not."

So much for sweet and sensitive.

"Daddy," Jennifer whined, "you've got to

make Lily change clothes before we get to the rink. Nobody wears their performance outfits to practice."

"I do," said Lily. "I look like a figure-skater princess."

"You're a cow!" Jennifer leaned around the seat to snarl. "I don't even want to be your sister."

"Daddy, make her stop."

Jennifer went louder. "She's sooo embarrassing."

Paul pulled onto the shoulder of the road and slammed the car into Park. He took a sip of black coffee from a thermal mug that never managed to keep the liquid hotter than tepid. From the CD player came the music that Jennifer was using for her latest figure-skating routine. "I Enjoy Being a Girl."

"We can't stop here," Jennifer said desperately. "We're going to be late. Again."

"We got to hurry," Lily echoed. "I have to practice my double axel."

"You wish! You can't do a double."

"Can too."

"Not. Not. Not."

Not for the first time, Paul wished his daughters had been interested in a sport he could get excited about. Skiing or rock climbing or mountain biking. If they had to strap on ice skates, why the hell couldn't they play hockey?

He waited until the car was quiet except for the perky music from the CD, then aimed a stern look at Jennifer, whose rosebud mouth pulled down in a frown. "Don't ever say that you don't want to be Lily's sister."

"But she's—"

"Never say it. We're family. You. Me. And Lily."

"And Mommy," Jennifer added.

"Right." Wherever Mommy was. His ex-wife had taken off before Lily was out of diapers and didn't stay in touch. "We're family. Understand?"

"I guess." She flung herself against the seat and stared straight ahead through the windshield.

He peered into the rear where Lily, the self-proclaimed princess, plucked at the silver spangles on the leotard she wore under her parka. "Why are you wearing your fancy outfit to practice?"

"Coach Megan wanted to see it before to-night."

"Show it to her, then change into your

other clothes. I don't want those sparkles to get ruined." That scrap of fabric had cost a pretty penny. "Promise you'll do that."

"Yes, Daddy."

He nodded. "Both of you. No more fighting."

"Daddy?" Jennifer was still scowling. "Is Mommy coming to our performance tonight?"

"She lives in Texas, honey. That's a long way from here. Besides, I'll be there." His presence felt insufficient.

"Who's going to help me put on my makeup?"

"You're wearing makeup?"

The girls exchanged a glance and rolled their eyes. "Everybody wears makeup for performance," Jennifer informed him.

"I'll take care of it," Paul said as he merged back onto the road and drove the last couple of miles to the new indoor ice-skating rink. He waited until the girls had scampered inside. After skating practice, they were scheduled for an all-day play date with a friend, another little ice-skating princess.

Paul had to work today. And, apparently, he also had to figure out a way to get lipstick and mascara on his girls. He shuddered at the thought.

Wheeling around in the parking lot, he headed back toward home. There was just enough time to grab a shower, change into his uniform and report for duty. After he checked in, his first order of business would be filling out reports on the five people he'd interviewed at Julia's place—a waste of time. All five came from the Washington, D.C., area, but none of them recognized John Maser's name.

Though Paul had suspicions about these people, he'd have to wait for more evidence before pursuing this investigation further. John Maser's accident could have been just that—an unfortunate vehicular accident.

Still, that single dying word kept repeating in Paul's brain. *Murder.*

As he pulled up in front of his house, his cell phone rang, and he picked up. Immediately, he recognized Julia's rich, alto voice. She sounded agitated.

"Paul, I need for you to come here. Right away."

"What's wrong?"

"I can't explain. Just come. Please."

If she'd been anybody else, he would

have insisted on more details. But he liked that she'd called him. He wanted to be the knight in shining armor who could solve all her problems. "I'll be there in twenty-five minutes."

JULIA HAD NEVER BEEN in such a complicated situation. The general was dead. He was in his locked bedroom, all alone with the gun in his hand. He'd left a suicide note.

Yet, she knew in her heart that his death was murder.

Her duty as a federal agent was to encourage an investigation. But if the local law enforcement got involved, her safehouse would be exposed. She'd have no choice but to recommend closing down the entire operation, and she didn't want that to happen. She was proud of her work here and loved the mountains. The safehouse felt more like home than anywhere she'd ever lived, and she'd do anything to protect it. Even if it meant misleading Paul.

When she opened the front door for him, she forced herself to look him in the eye. Inside her rib cage her heart was jumping like a jackrabbit, but she kept her voice steady, "Thank you for coming."

"No problem." As he stepped across the threshold, his gaze flicked around the room, taking in every detail. "What's up?"

"Come with me."

She led the way up the staircase to the second-floor bedrooms. Their boot heels echoed on the hardwood floor. She and Paul were almost alone in the house. Her so-called guests—the Homeland Security experts—were horseback riding as a team-building exercise. Julia had suggested that everybody lay low while the police were here.

Using her key, she opened the door to General Harrison Naylor's bedroom. The death scene was carefully arranged. Wearing his Marine dress blues, the general lay stretched out on the bed. In his right hand, he gripped his silver Colt Double Eagle pistol with sound suppressor attached. The fatal bullet had gone through the back of his skull, leaving his face unmarked. His eyes were closed. His life-blood stained the pillows and the linens.

On a small desk, his laptop was open but not turned on. A note rested beside it.

As Paul stepped gingerly into the scene, Julia told her first lie. "I found him like this."

When she first discovered the body, she had closed and relocked the bedroom door behind her. Standing over the body of the general, her FBI training kicked into high gear. Her brain cleared. Her priorities sorted. Much to her shame, her first thoughts centered on the security of the safehouse.

She forced herself to focus. A man was dead. A heroic military man. A man who led other brave Marines, like her brother, into battle. There were procedures to be followed.

Her trained gaze had gone to the rows of medals on this fallen soldier's chest. At that moment, she realized that the general had not committed suicide. The medals were not in proper order.

A Marine would never be so careless. When her brother was laid out in his coffin, she had studied the Marine Corps Manual to make sure his ribbons and medals were in correct alignment. The general would never make such a mistake. Therefore, she could assume that someone else had pinned those medals to his chest. This wasn't a suicide.

However, if the general was murdered, it meant a prolonged investigation by local authorities. A simple suicide would be an open-and-shut case. She could carefully escort the local lawmen through their duties without revealing the real business of the safehouse.

And so, she had decided to change the medals, putting them in proper order. As if this tampering with the crime scene wasn't bad enough, she'd done more.

Under the sink in the general's bathroom, she found a pair of latex gloves, slipped them on and returned to the body.

The general's shoes had been scuffed. A true Marine would never consider himself to be fully in uniform with dirty shoes. She'd removed the shoes from the general's feet, polished them and put them back on.

Guilt coursed through her veins like poison. How could she have done such a thing? Her life was dedicated to fighting crime, and she was no better than any other criminal, hiding evidence. How could she allow the general's family to believe that he'd killed himself?

She watched as Paul prowled around the bedroom, being careful not to touch anything. He leaned over the general's body for a closer look. "This is strange."

"What?" She halfway hoped that he'd see

through her tampering and confront her. "What's strange?"

"He's wearing his hearing aid," Paul said. "If I was going to shoot myself in the head, that would be the first thing to go."

Her lips pinched together, holding back an urge to confess to him. Not only was she guilty of rearranging a crime scene but she was also betraying Paul, deliberately misleading him.

He asked, "Was his bedroom door locked?"

"Yes." That much was true. "And we have a security camera in the hallway. I've already checked the tape. There was no one who came into or out of his room."

"A security camera?" He turned toward her. "Why?"

"Security," she said as if it were the most obvious thing in the world. Julia knew that most people in nearby Redding didn't even bother locking their doors. "There was already a lot of security equipment when I moved here."

"And you still keep it running?" he said. "Have you been bothered by theft? Vandalism?"

There wasn't much likelihood of anyone

sneaking up on the safehouse. If they came within a hundred feet of the property, they'd be met by armed agents.

"I've never had any problems," she said, trying to shrug off his questioning gaze. "The camera came in handy this time, right?"

Paul circled the bed, went to the window and glanced out at the eaves. Julia knew it was possible for the murderer to have come across the roof and entered the general's room through this window. Such an action would require the expert skill of a rock climber who was accustomed to clinging to tiny ledges. She'd immediately thought of Gil Bradley, the former Navy SEAL who had the look and the manner of an assassin.

If Gil had murdered the general, she didn't want to shield him from justice. But she had to keep her secret; she couldn't let people know this was an FBI safehouse.

Paul inspected the double-paned window. The lower half was designed to be pulled up over the upper half in summer to let in the fresh air. "This window doesn't have a lock."

"There's no way to open it from the outside without prying it loose."

"After the sheriff gets here, I'll need to check it out."

"Surely, you don't think someone crept in here during the night and murdered the general."

She held her breath, waiting for his response.

"I doubt it," he said. "There are no signs of a struggle. It appears that the general was shot where he lies because there aren't blood spatters in the rest of the room."

"So it's suicide," she said.

"Apparent suicide," Paul corrected her. "We still need to go through the drill. Taking fingerprints. Checking the room for fibers, hairs and tiny spots of blood. I'll need to interview your guests to see if any of them heard or saw anything unusual."

"I'd really appreciate if this could be handled with as little fuss as possible. It's bad for business and—" She paused midsentence. Her gaze turned to the dead man. How could she be scheming in his presence? "God, I sound cold. I shouldn't be thinking about business."

"I understand," Paul said.

"My other guests knew the general. I don't want to upset them any more than necessary."

"They'll probably call off their meeting," Paul said.

That was what she had expected. But the senator had been adamant about moving forward with their mission; he had no other free time in his schedule. "They've decided to carry on."

Clearly taken aback, Paul said, "Doesn't sound like your other guests are concerned about the general's suicide."

"They're task-oriented people from Washington. It's not up to me to approve or disapprove of their decision."

Her job was to keep them safe. And she'd failed miserably. As she glanced at the lifeless body stretched out on the bed, her heart ached with the weight of her guilty secrets. *I'm sorry, General. So horribly sorry.* He deserved to have his death investigated. Suicide was looked upon as the coward's way out. A Marine deserved better.

She felt Paul's arm encircle her shoulders. Gently, he guided her toward the bedroom door. "Don't worry, Julia. I'll take care of everything. We'll be as discreet as possible."

Standing in the hallway outside the

bedroom, she allowed herself to accept his comforting embrace, leaning her head into the crook of his neck. Her arms wrapped around his huge torso. He was so big and solid.

Though his touch was in no way inappropriate and he patted her shoulders in an almost impersonal manner, she felt a surge of erotic tension. Her breasts rubbed against his chest. She inhaled his masculine scent. Gazing up, she noticed that his chin was marked with morning stubble. Though he was in his deputy uniform, he had to have come here immediately without even stopping to shave.

He was anxious to help, and she repaid him with lies, using him for her own purposes. Julia stepped away from his embrace. There was a depth of meaning in her voice when she whispered, "I'm sorry."

"No need for you to be sorry. This isn't your fault."

If only he knew what she'd done. In his warm brown eyes, she saw the glow of kindness. She didn't merit his friendship. "What happens next?"

"I'll call the sheriff. He's not going to be happy. Two fatalities in two days."

"Is that unusual?"

"Not for a city," Paul said. "But we're a fairly quiet little county."

"I hate to bring this up," she said, "but there will be media attention. General Naylor was well known. He did commentary on a lot of news programs."

"Which means the sheriff is going to be talking to the press," Paul said. "He can handle it."

She envisioned television trucks with satellite dishes and reporters with microphones. A nightmare! "I really don't want my lodge to be the backdrop for those interviews."

"No problem. We'll evacuate the body to the hospital before autopsy. The sheriff can make his statement to the press from that location."

For that, she was endlessly grateful. The last thing she needed was a mob of curious interviewers crawling all over the safehouse.

"Yesterday," Paul said, "the general reacted strangely when you mentioned his television commentaries. What did he say? Something about not believing everything you hear. It was like he thought he was being unfairly criticized."

"Paranoid," she said. "That fits with suicide, doesn't it?"

"Did you notice anything else unusual about his state of mind?"

"Other than shooting at rabbits off the deck behind the lodge?"

"Strange behavior," he said.

"But not typical. The general kept to himself. He got here a day ahead of the others and spent most of that time in his room."

Paul glanced down at his boots, then looked up at her again. "How much do you know about makeup? You know, lipstick and stuff."

That question came out of the blue. "On occasion, I've been known to use cosmetics."

"You don't need that stuff," he said quickly. "I like the way you look. Healthy. And your eyes…well, your blue eyes are beautiful."

His gruff compliment took her off guard. Had he really said that she was beautiful? Her eyes were beautiful? Self-consciously, she glanced away. "Thank you."

"This is about my two daughters. They have an ice-skating performance tonight at the rink near Vail, and they need to put on makeup. That happens to be a topic I don't know much about."

She peeked up at him. Though he was trying to scowl, the dimples in his cheeks deepened. Adorable. "I'd like to help you, Paul."

He waved his hand back and forth as if to erase his words. "Forget it. You have enough to worry about."

"Tell you what. I'll put together a little makeup kit for you to take with you."

"Thanks a lot, Julia."

His gratitude was utterly sincere. The sheepish expression on his face almost brought her to tears. For the first time in her life, Julia had purposely done wrong. She was lying to this terrific guy, and it was tearing her apart.

Unable to look in Paul's trusting eyes for one more second, she pivoted and headed down the staircase.

In the kitchen, they found Craig Lennox, the other FBI agent who worked with her at the safehouse. Craig, a computer expert, was nearly as concerned as Julia about the true purpose of the safehouse being discovered. The office on the basement floor—filled with high-tech surveillance and computer equipment—was his domain, and he didn't want anybody touching anything.

His dark eyes darted nervously in his thin face. He nodded to Paul, who he'd met yesterday. "Is there anything I should be doing?"

"Sit tight," Julia said. "The police will be here soon."

He held up a videocassette. "I made copies of the surveillance tapes that show the hallway outside the general's room."

"For all night?" Paul asked.

"From eleven o'clock when the general went to bed until this morning when Julia opened his door."

"Nobody entered the room?"

"Nobody," Craig said. "These tapes are time coded on the bottom. There's not one second missing."

Paul took a cell phone from his utility belt and punched in a number on his cell phone. "Jurisdiction can be complicated up here, but your resort is well outside Vail's city limits so the Eagle County sheriff will be handling this incident. There's no need to call in the state investigators for a suicide."

A suicide. Paul seemed convinced. She could only hope that the other county officials would also be satisfied by that explanation.

Chapter Four

That evening at half past five o'clock when Paul herded everybody out of the house, the girls were wearing their sparkly costumes under their parkas. Their black hair was done up in curly ponytails, and their makeup was perfect thanks to makeup kits assembled by Julia and expert help from Abby Nelson. Abby was an FBI agent recently assigned to the Denver office so she could be near Mac Granger, a homicide detective, who was one of Paul's oldest and best friends.

Earlier today, Paul had called Mac and asked if he and Abby would drive up to Redding for the performance that night. "It would mean a lot to Jennifer and Lily."

"Count on us," Mac said.

Though it wasn't the same as having their mother attend, Paul knew the girls would be pleased to have a decent-sized cheering section in the audience.

Another good friend, Jess Isler, was also coming along. Jess had been staying with Paul while recuperating from a serious injury. Being with Jess—a ladies' man—usually meant there were several adoring females in the vicinity. Jess was on the Vail ski patrol and was so ridiculously handsome that he regularly dated the supermodels and movie stars who showed up on the slopes. Right now, however, Jess seemed to be spending a lot of one-on-one time with a nurse from the hospital who had promised to meet them at the rink.

Paul looked over the entourage. "We should take two cars."

Jennifer batted her eyelashes. "Me and Lily want to ride with Abby."

Teasing, Jess clutched his heart. "You don't want to ride with me? I'm hurt."

"We see you every day." Jennifer had already linked her hand with Abby's. "Mac and Abby drove all the way up here from Denver to watch us skate."

"But we love you, Jessy-Messy," Lily said happily. Her lipstick was already smeared. "You go with Daddy."

"If I don't see you before the show," Jess said, "break a leg."

Lily gasped. "Huh?"

"That means good luck," Jess said. "It's an expression. Break a leg means—"

"Everybody knows that," Jennifer said. "Come on, Lily."

When Paul got behind the wheel of the Explorer, he surreptitiously watched as Jess climbed into the passenger seat. Six weeks ago, Jess had been shot in the chest. For a while, Paul was as scared as hell, afraid his friend wasn't going to make it. Though he wasn't a particularly religious man, he'd prayed hard and long. Jess and Mac had grown up together; they were closer to him than brothers.

So far, Jess's recovery seemed to be going well, but he wasn't back to full strength, and he had a bad habit of overexerting himself. That habit was the main reason Paul had insisted that Jess stay with him in Redding even though he owned a condo in Vail. Though it was driving Jess crazy to know there was fresh snow and mountains to be skied, Paul kept him safely on the sidelines.

Jess slammed the car door and turned to

Paul. He was pale but grinning. "Where did you get the lipstick?"

"I have my ways." Paul quickly changed the subject. "You had therapy today. How are you doing?"

"The doc said I could try skiing next week, but I have to wear this girdle contraption to protect my busted ribs." He cocked an eyebrow. "The lipstick?"

"A lady friend."

"I knew it," he crowed. "Who is she?"

"Forget it." Paul pulled out of the drive and led the way so Mac could follow. "I'm not going to introduce you. Because she'd be all gaga over your skinny butt."

"Don't go there, Paul. I'm doing my best to convince Marcia that I'm not a hound dog."

"Getting serious about her? Maybe thinking about marriage?"

"Whoa, buddy. Marcia and I haven't even been, you know, intimate."

Paul offered wry condolence. "Poor you. I guess it's complicated to make love with broken ribs."

"It's been almost six weeks. That's the longest time I've gone without since we were in high school."

"A little abstinence is good for you," Paul said. "If you decide to marry Marcia, it's going to be a day of mourning for the other women of Eagle County."

"You're full of crap."

"Not really."

Paul was a realist. He'd never been popular with women. In spite of his size—or maybe because of it—he tended to be shy. Then, when he finally spoke, he'd blurt out something stupid. Around women, he was clumsy, always tripping over his own big feet.

All the way from grade school to high school graduation when he, Jess and Mac had been best pals, the girls had flocked around handsome Jess with his streaked blond hair and blue eyes. Mac's relationships tended to be more monogamous and intense. And Paul was relegated to the role of the perpetual fifth wheel.

It was ironic that he'd been the first one to settle down into a marriage and have kids. And unfortunate that the marriage had fallen apart in spite of his best efforts to hold things together.

"Come on," Jess said, "tell me who gave you the lipstick."

"Her name is Julia Last, and she runs that resort where Mac stayed when he was in town."

"Did you ask her out?"

"Dinner. Next week." Paul figured he might as well take advantage of Jess's vast dating expertise. "Where should I take her?"

"That depends. Tell me about her."

"She's strong." That was the first word that came to mind when he thought of Julia. "The first time I saw her, she was chopping wood, handling an ax like a lumberjack. But that's not to say she's masculine. She's got long curly brown hair that smells great. And the prettiest blue eyes I've ever seen. She's tall. With an hourglass figure. Full, round hips and full, round..."

His voice trailed off as a picture of Julia took shape in his mind. Throughout this morning's investigation with the sheriff, the coroner and the ambulance team that removed General Harrison Naylor's body, he hadn't been able to take his eyes off her. Though she'd obviously been tense, he admired her composure as she served up coffee and muffins all around.

Julia only relaxed after the forensics were done and the sheriff agreed with Paul's conclusion that the general's death was a suicide. The note he'd left behind stated his regrets for wrong decisions he'd made in the heat of battle.

"What does she like doing?" Jess asked.

"There are horses at the lodge." He took a moment to imagine Julia on horseback with her hair flying loose around her shoulders. A very sexy image. "She likes football, but prefers hockey."

"Just like you."

"When I'm around her," Paul said, "I want to tell her everything about me and the girls. Every little detail. At the same time, it's nice to just be near her. She's a woman who knows how to be quiet."

"You've got it bad," Jess said. "Here's what you do on the first date. Order a catered picnic basket and pick up some decent wine. Then you charter a plane. I know I guy who flies for cheap. And then—"

"What? Charter a plane?"

"Think big. You want to impress the woman."

"I don't want her to think I'm abducting her," Paul said.

"Women like a man who takes control and sweeps them off their feet."

Paul's instincts told him that Julia wouldn't appreciate a lot of fuss. "I think a simple dinner is going to be enough."

He pulled into the parking lot outside the ice-skating rink, met up with the others and escorted the girls into the backstage area. The new skating rink had been a huge success with lots of kids interested. Backstage, a couple of dozen skaters, ranging in age from five years old to high school, were doing stretch exercises and giggling wildly. There were few other men in this preparation area and Paul made a hasty retreat after wishing Jennifer and Lily good luck.

He returned to the bleachers surrounding the rink. From the way Mac and Abby were smirking, he guessed that Jess had blabbed to them about Julia. Swell.

GUILT HAD DRIVEN Julia from the safehouse. After sitting at the dinner table with the others who had known General Harrison Naylor and had offered respectful toasts to his memory, she had to leave. How could she have tampered with the crime scene? How could she, in good conscience, allow the world to believe this brave old Marine had committed suicide?

She needed to confess, and that need lead her to the ice-skating rink near Vail where she knew she would find Deputy Paul Hemmings. She hoped that he would understand, that he wouldn't hate her for what she'd done. Inside the arena, she took a seat by herself on the bleachers and watched as these seemingly delicate skaters performed their athletic spins and leaps.

Checking out the audience, she immediately spotted Paul. Unfortunately, he was with Mac Granger and Abby Nelson—two people who knew about the safehouse. No way could Julia face them. It had been a mistake to come here.

As she rose from her seat, intending to slip away before she was noticed, Paul spotted her. He bolted from his seat and came toward her. She couldn't run away, had to face him.

He took a seat on the bleachers beside her. His huge thigh brushed against hers. "I'm glad to see you, Julia."

"Did you get the girl's makeup put on straight?"

"Abby did it." He pointed back toward the others who were all staring in their direction. "Abby Nelson. I think you know her. And Mac."

"Yes." Julia gave them a small wave. "They stayed with me. How are they doing?"

"Good. They've got a good relationship. I've never seen Mac so open."

They sat quietly for a moment and watched the tiniest skaters go through a simple routine with only a couple of slip-ups. Julia's anxiety ratcheted higher with each passing second. In spite of the cold from the ice, she was sweating. Her mouth was dry as cotton. Her feet were itching to run.

"Something wrong?" Paul asked.

She had to face up to what she'd done. "Could I talk to you in private for a minute?"

They climbed down from the bleachers and went toward the area where hot dogs and pretzels were being sold to benefit the Eagle County Skaters. From what Julia had heard, this newly built facility was a tremendous success—booked solid with figure-skating lessons, hockey teams and recreational time. She wished she could enjoy the evening, but the cheers from the audience only heightened her tension. She knew that once she spoke out, her words could never be reclaimed. The secrecy of the safehouse would be in Paul's hands. "Can I trust you?"

"A hundred percent."

"Even if I might tell you something that could cause conflict with your job?"

He gave her a friendly little pat on the shoulder. "I guess that depends. If you tell me you've got twenty dead bodies buried in your backyard, I'll probably have to dig them up."

She'd expected that response. Paul was a deputy, sworn to defend the law. And so was she. "It's about the resort."

"I'm listening."

"My resort offers something more than lodging and meals." She bit her lip. *Now or never. Just tell him.* "I'm running an FBI safehouse."

"You're an FBI agent?"

"Yes."

He didn't seem surprised in the least. Instead, his expression was visibly more relaxed. "That's a relief."

"You suspected something?"

"You've got surveillance cameras all over the damn place, and your employees wear shoulder holsters. Mac was real secretive about the resort when he was staying there."

He grinned, showing his dimples. "I was worried that you might be protecting a bad secret."

"Twenty bodies buried in the backyard?"

"Something like that."

"Nobody else can know about this."

"Understood. A safehouse isn't much good if everybody knows it's there." He took both her hands in his and gave a squeeze. "Don't worry, Julia. Your secret is safe with me."

Suddenly, his head jerked up. "That's Jennifer's music. Come on, we have to see her routine."

As they hustled back to the rink, her emotions were in turmoil. She'd taken the first step toward the truth. Would Paul be equally sanguine with her confession about tampering with crime-scene evidence?

The music was "I Enjoy Being a Girl." Four slender young skaters, dressed in pink-sequined leotards with short skirts, took the ice. Holding hands they skated in a figure eight.

"The one in front," Paul said, "that's my Jennifer."

"I can tell." Jennifer had her father's black

hair and dark eyes. And his dimples. "She looks like you."

"God, I hope not."

She glanced up at his profile. Every bit of his attention focused on the ice as he watched the skaters glide to the center. Each did a spin. Then a spread-eagle leap. After his Jennifer successfully completed her double axel, Paul gave a cheer and pumped his fist. "She did it. Damn, I'm glad. There'd be no living with the girl if she slipped up."

He applauded enthusiastically as the routine completed and the skaters left the ice, then he turned to Julia. "That's all for my kids until the grand finale. Can I buy you a hot dog?"

She nodded, wishing that she could relax and share the joy of this proud father. Though Paul was a deputy who carried a gun and dealt with crime, everything about him seemed wonderfully sane and normal—the very opposite of her daily routine.

At the safehouse, there was constant surveillance, the ever-present threat of danger. She was always looking over her shoulder. Especially now, with her suspicion that the general had been murdered.

She slathered mustard on a fat bratwurst

and took a healthy bite, which she immediately regretted. Her throat was too tight to swallow. And her stomach twisted in a knot.

Forcing herself to gulp down the brat, Julia realized that she had to be really, truly upset if she was having trouble eating. Usually, she had a cast-iron stomach. "Paul, there's something else."

"Okay." He led her to a round table, and gallantly held her chair while she sat.

Though there was no one nearby, she lowered her voice. "It's about the general. I have reason to believe he was murdered."

"Tell me why."

She hesitated. Supposedly, confession was good for the soul. But she hated admitting what she'd done. Throughout her career with the FBI, she'd been an exemplary agent. No mistakes. No black marks on her record.

Quietly, Paul said, "All the evidence points to suicide. The door to the general's bedroom was locked. Your surveillance tapes show that no one entered or exited. We checked the window, and it showed no sign of tampering. There were other fingerprints in the room, but none on the gun. No sign of a struggle. No blood spatters to indicate he was shot somewhere else, then laid out on the bed."

"I know," she said miserably.

"Only one of your guests, Senator Ashbrook, who had the room right next to the general, reported hearing anything unusual. A thud that could have been the gunshot with the silencer. That was around midnight."

She nodded.

"Those are the facts, Julia. Nobody else was in that room with the general. Nobody else pulled that trigger."

For a moment, she doubted her own suspicions. Everything Paul said was correct. It seemed physically impossible for the general to have been murdered. She set the bratwurst on the paper plate. "Maybe I'm wrong."

"If I had to guess," Paul said, "I'd say you were feeling guilty that he died on your watch."

That thought hadn't occurred to Julia. Her feelings of failure about having the general commit suicide at the safehouse might have caused her to make too much of her observations. A couple of misplaced medals and scuffed shoes didn't override all the other evidence. "What about the note?"

"It seemed like a straightforward apology," Paul said. "He felt bad about mistakes he'd made in battle."

"It was a printed out page from his laptop."

"But he signed it." Paul pointed to her bratwurst. "Not hungry?"

"I guess not."

"Do you mind if I finish that off for you?"

"Go right ahead." She liked watching him eat. A big man with big appetites. No problem was too large for him to handle. When she was with him, her burden of responsibility seemed lighter. "Thanks, Paul. You've put my mind at ease."

He finished off her bratwurst and grinned. "Would you like to go back to the ice and join the others? I'm sure Mac and Abby would like to say hello."

She shook her head. "I've already been gone too long. I don't want any more trouble tonight."

"Are you expecting problems?"

"Not really. The others knew the general well. Over dinner, they were subdued. Not sad enough to cancel their meetings, though." She rose from the table. "Good night, Paul."

"I'll walk you out to your car."

Though it wasn't necessary for him to escort her, she appreciated the gesture. At the exit from the rink, he held the door for her, and she realized how long it had been since anyone had treated her like a lady.

To the other agents at the safehouse, she was the boss. Her gender didn't matter. And her "guests" treated her like a function—somebody who was there to facilitate their needs.

In contrast, Paul was gentlemanly and courteous, taking her arm to guide her through the parking lot. She wanted desperately to believe he was right about the general's death. It was suicide. No one else was in the room. It had to be suicide.

When they reached her car, she turned toward him. Her head tilted back. She had to look up to gaze into his face, dimly lit by the lights in the skating rink parking lot.

"You should get back inside," she said. "It's cold out here."

"That's strange. I feel nice and warm."

So did she. The comforting warmth that radiated inside her held the December cold at bay.

"I'm glad you came to me, Julia."

"Me, too." His calm statement of the facts

had gone a long way toward reassuring her. Impulsively, she reached up and rested her hand on his cheek.

He responded in kind. His hand glided along her jawline and rested at her nape under her ponytail. He leaned closer, and she knew he intended to kiss her. She wanted him to.

Their noses rubbed. His mouth brushed lightly against hers. His lips tasted of mustard, and she was hungry—hungry for him. His gentle kiss left her longing for more. But he stepped away, hesitant and shy.

His voice was husky. "I might have to stop by your place tomorrow. You know, to follow up."

"I'll be there."

"Not that I think the general's death was murder," he said.

"Probably not," she agreed.

"If it was," he said with a frown, "that would mean the murderer was one of the people staying at the house."

A shudder went through her. "All my guests would be in danger."

"And you," he said.

With all her heart, she hoped he was wrong.

Chapter Five

The next day when Julia sat down to lunch with the four remaining participants in the Homeland Security project, she remembered Paul's words. One of these people might be a murderer. They certainly looked angry enough. The hostility around the long table in the dining room was palpable. They sat where she had laid the plates—two on each side with Julia at the head of the table.

Senator Marcus Ashbrook poked his fork into his salad. "Is this lettuce organic?"

"It doesn't matter," said RJ Katz. Her sleek helmet of calico-colored hair fell forward, hiding her delicate features. "Lettuce approved by the FDA isn't going to kill you."

"I'm with Ashbrook," said Gil Bradley. His body was his temple. "I want fresh, organic produce."

He glared accusingly at Julia who said, "As a matter of fact, all our produce is certified free from artificial additives or pesticides. We purchase from the same source as one of the exclusive Vail hotels."

Ashbrook was appeased for the moment. He took a bite, chewed thoroughly and swallowed. "What about the chicken?"

"Free range." Because the safehouse budget for food was subsidized by the FBI, she was able to buy the highest quality. Unlike other struggling little resorts, she was under no pressure to turn a profit. Julia's pressures were different and more deadly.

Gil glanced across the table at David Dillard, the computer expert. "What's our agenda for this afternoon?"

"I need to reprogram the simulation exercise," David said. "It was originally set up for input from five people."

"We agreed," Gil said, "that I would take the general's position. My background as a Navy SEAL qualifies me to speak to the military view."

"My simulation doesn't work that way," David said. "I present you all with a Homeland Security situation, and you need to concentrate on your own responses. Political from the senator. FBI and financial from RJ. And the CIA response from you, Gil."

"What happens to the military response?" Ashbrook asked. "We need to know what the generals would require."

"I'll program in the most likely response." David pushed his glasses up on the bridge of his nose. "It's not a perfect solution, but the alternative is to cancel the entire exercise."

"That's not an option," Ashbrook said. "General Naylor would have wanted us to continue."

"You don't know that." RJ's wide catlike eyes narrowed. "None of us can guess what was going through the general's mind."

"We were close," said the senator. "The general and I served on two other committees together."

"Then maybe you can tell us," RJ said. "Why did he kill himself?"

"My dear young lady, you have no idea of the pressures that come from great responsibilities."

"None of us can guess what he was thinking," Gil said. Though he seemed an unlikely peacemaker, his tone was placating. "We can only mourn his passing."

There was a moment of silence as they attacked their food. They almost seemed sad, and Julia was glad for this small show of humanity from this group.

"The general's absence," David said, "doesn't ruin the project. Our purpose here is to create a prototype for communication."

"Waste of time," Ashbrook muttered. "I can already tell you what you're going to learn from these computer simulations."

"What might that be?" David asked.

"It's obvious. The first response to a Homeland Security situation is the need for leadership. One man." Ashbrook held up his index finger. "One acknowledged leader."

"That might well be our conclusion," David said. "Unfortunately, when there's a threat to national security, several branches of government are involved."

Ashbrook returned his attention to his food. "I fully intend to lead this first response team when it is organized."

"Do you?" RJ's voice was cool. "Why should you be the leader?"

"That's what I do." Ashbrook jabbed a fork across the table in her direction. "I lead."

"I always thought the job of a senator was to represent the interests of his state."

"It's within the interests of Wyoming to deal with Homeland Security."

"Right," RJ muttered. "As if Wyoming is a major target for international terrorism."

As Julia watched their sniping, she wondered if this power struggle might be a motive for murder. The general—another man who was accustomed to being the leader—would have been a formidable adversary for Ashbrook.

"In any case," David said, "I'd appreciate if we could take a break after lunch so I can work out the bugs in my program. Maybe start up again around two-thirty."

There were murmurs of agreement around the table. RJ added, "There's no need for more team building. Right?"

"Certainly not," Ashbrook said.

From the atmosphere of tension evident around the dining table, Julia guessed that the exercises designed to build trust and co-operation among these people had been a dismal failure. They were all too high-powered, too focused on their own agendas, their own secrets.

She offered, "If any of you would like to

use the time off for recreation, I can arrange horseback riding."

When they all refused, she was relieved. The less time she spent with these people, the better.

AS IT TURNED OUT, Paul had a legitimate, police-oriented reason for visiting Julia's resort. He needed to talk with the senator in conjunction with his investigation into the vehicular death of John Maser.

A background check on the deceased man had revealed some interesting information. He had started out as one of the good guys and received an honorable discharge from the Marines. Then his life went to hell. His rap sheet showed three arrests and one conviction on fraud. His primary activities involved gunrunning and dealing in illegal weaponry. Currently, he was in touch with a survivalist group based in Wyoming. That fact formed a tenuous connection to the Wyoming senator who was staying at Julia's place.

When he parked in front, Paul saw the pretty little resort through a new focus. This was an FBI safehouse where protected witnesses were secreted away and surveillance was high.

The agent who opened the door at the safehouse, Roger Flannery, informed Paul that the guests were resting and Julia was with the horses. *No problem!* Paul would much rather talk to her, anyway. He left the front porch and followed a well-worn path around the house to the barn.

Though the sun was shining and the temperature was in the low forties, misty gray clouds smeared across the skies. The forecasters were calling for major snowfall tonight. Not that anybody took those predictions too seriously. Colorado weather was notoriously fickle. His buddy, Jess, described the sudden changes in temperature and precipitation as Rocky Mountain PMS—ranging from heat wave to ice storm in a matter of minutes.

In the heated barn, Paul found Julia saddling up a dappled mare. She wore a short leather jacket, giving him an enticing view of her voluptuous bottom in snug-fitting Levi's.

He glanced over his shoulder toward the safehouse, wondering if they were being observed on surveillance cameras right now. If he reached out and patted her butt, would the other agents at the house have a front row view?

Hands in pockets, he looked back toward Julia. "Going for a ride?"

"A short ride," she said.

He leaned close to her and whispered, "Are we being watched right now?"

"We have a camera in the barn, but it's not turned on right now. During the day, we rely on sensors in the fence surrounding the property to let us know if anybody is approaching."

"So nobody would know if I did this." He glided his hand down her arm, caught her hand and squeezed lightly.

"Nobody's watching," she said.

"Or this?" He gave a little tug, pulling her closer to him. "Nobody would know."

"No one but me." She slipped into his arms for an embrace. Though her lovely face tilted up toward him and her smile was welcoming, she moved away before he could kiss her. "Do you ride, Paul?"

"Hell, yes." Though his arms were empty, the fresh scent of her hair tantalized his senses.

"Come with me."

"You bet."

In minutes, he'd saddled a big black stallion with a blaze of white on his chest.

Together, he and Julia led their horses from the heated barn and mounted.

"What's my horse's name?" he asked.

"Diablo."

"The devil. Bad temper?"

"Not at all. Most of these horses are gentle, accustomed to being ridden by strangers. I do have a pregnant mare who's really cranky. Poor thing."

On horseback, Julia was as striking as he'd imagined. She sat tall in the saddle with shoulders back. The cool December wind brought roses to her cheeks, making her blue eyes look even more beautiful.

Last night, Jess had teased him about having a bad case of the hots for her, and he was dead right. Paul couldn't find a single flaw in this woman.

He rode beside her. "Mac and Abby say hi."

"They seem to have a good relationship," she said. "I'm glad."

"They have a lot in common with both of them being involved in law enforcement." *Like us,* he wanted to add.

"There's a lot of stress that goes along with their work," she said. "Especially for Abby. She was undercover a lot. That's hard."

"Have you ever done undercover work?"

"I'm not the right personality type." She tossed her head, sending a ripple through her long, brown ponytail. "I've never been good at lying."

"But you've kept the safehouse a secret for a couple of years."

"Keeping a secret is different than out-and-out lying. Until yesterday, nobody paid much attention to this little resort. And then, when I was under pressure…" Her blue eyes focused on him. "I had to tell you."

"I'm glad you did. I wouldn't like having a lie between us."

When they reached the open meadow, both horses were frisky, tossing their heads and tugging at the reins. They seemed to know that this was their time to run hard.

Julia pointed to a distant outcropping of jagged boulders shaped like the head of a rabbit with two ears sticking straight up. "I'll meet you there."

Leaning forward in the saddle, she made a clicking noise. With her heels, she gave her mare a nudge. The horse took off in a shot, leaving Paul and the stallion behind.

He flicked his reins. "Let's go, boy."

Diablo charged forward. His powerful

sinews flexed and extended as they flew across the open land, closing the gap between himself and Julia.

The exhilarating sensation of speed shot through him like a jolt of electricity. Paul loved going fast whether it was downhill skiing, racing a car or riding a stallion. The wind swirled in their wake. The arid landscape, dotted with snow, flashed in his peripheral vision.

Though Julia had a head start, Paul reached the outcropping at the same time she did. Pulling back on the reins, he announced, "It's a tie."

"This wasn't a race," she scoffed. "If we'd been racing, there's no way you would have caught me."

"I'd have won," he said. "My horse is bigger than yours."

"It's not about size."

"Too bad. I'm usually the biggest guy around."

"I'll bet you are."

They rode side by side at the edge of the forest. Though the ground was dry, there were still patches of unmelted snow. The white-trunked aspen had lost their golden autumn leaves, and the shrubs were bare. "I like winter," he said. "Everything gets quiet and still."

"And dead."

"Just resting. Building up strength for the springtime." He relaxed in the saddle, enjoying the rhythm of the stallion's gait. It had been a while since he'd gone horseback riding. "Now that you've had some time to think about it, how are you feeling about the general's death?"

"If it was murder, I couldn't have hand-picked a more suspicious bunch than my so-called guests. They're at one another's throats, especially the senator. He wants to be leader of this group. That could be a motive for murder."

"How so?"

"The general would have threatened his claim to leadership. Senator Ashbrook is hoping these meetings will result in an important position, something he could use to further his plan to be president." She shuddered. "I hate to think of that man running our country."

"He's the reason for my visit today," he said. "The guy who was killed in the car accident is suspected of supplying illegal weapons to a survivalist group in the senator's home state."

"You think Ashbrook has something to do with that?"

"Maybe." He shrugged. "Or he might be able to give me some info on the survivalists."

"Good luck finding out anything from him. He's as slippery as a..." She paused, trying to find the right word. "Slippery as a politician."

It worried him that Julia hadn't completely given up on her suspicions of murder. Did she know something she hadn't told him? "Let's suppose the senator does have a motive. How could he commit the crime?"

"I've thought about that," she said. "What if the killer knocked the general unconscious, then laid him out on the bed and pulled the trigger. The bullet wound would destroy evidence of being hit on the head."

"That still doesn't explain how the killer got into and out of the room."

"I know," she said.

"And the medical examiner would find evidence of a prior contusion."

The general was scheduled for autopsy today so his body could be released to his family for burial. Very likely, John Maser's autopsy would also be done today, though nobody was clamoring for his remains.

These two deceased men were unlikely partners in death. The general was a hero. John Maser was, from all that Paul had learned, a thug.

Both bodies had been transported to the medical examiner in Denver where they had the facilities for a sophisticated analysis. The Eagle County coroner had been glad to see them go.

Julia looked across the meadow toward the safehouse. "We should head back if you want to catch the senator before this afternoon's meetings start."

"What kind of meetings are these?" Paul asked.

"I'm not really sure. And I couldn't tell you if I was. The whole point of meeting here is secrecy."

"Understood."

"Paul, I'd appreciate if you didn't let on that I told you about the safehouse. Not even to Roger and Craig."

"Got it." He nodded. "Should we race back?"

Her blue-eyed gaze appraised him and the big, black stallion. "You're on. Go."

They took off together, their horses neck in neck. When Paul glanced over at her, he was distracted by her profile and the way she leaned forward in the saddle. But he kept up the pressure.

The gentlemanly thing would be to let her win. But he was pushing as hard as he could. Second place was never good enough.

They arrived at the fence at the same moment.

"I win," Julia said.

"In your dreams. I got here first."

She laughed as she guided her mare to the barn. "There's no shame in losing to a woman."

"No shame at all. Because I didn't lose."

"I guess we'll have to race again to see who's the clear winner."

"Guess so."

Next time meant he'd be seeing her again, and he was glad to settle for that solution.

SMILING TO HERSELF, Julia took the reins and led the horses into the barn while Paul went inside to catch the senator before the meeting started.

After she removed the saddles, she shooed

the horses they had ridden into the attached corral along with two other dappled geldings. Julia decided to keep Stormy, the pregnant mare, in her stall. Stormy had been skittish lately, and the vet said they should keep her quiet.

"How are you doing, Stormy?" Julia leaned into the stall. "Feeling okay?"

The mare's nostrils flared. She pawed the hay-covered floor of her stall. Her eyes were angry, impatient. This horse did not like being pregnant.

When Julia reached out toward her, the chestnut-colored horse nipped at her hand. Julia backed off. There were plenty of other jobs in the barn—hauling the saddles to the tack room, mucking out the other stalls, breaking open a fresh bale of hay.

As she worked, Julia's mind was busy. Her thoughts of the general's murder segued to a vision of Paul on Diablo. Most people were dwarfed by the size of that big, black horse. Not Paul. The breadth of his shoulders and the span of his thighs were perfect for Diablo. Paul's thick, black hair was the same color as the stallion's coat.

She heard a noise and stood up straight. "Who's there?"

Was that a mewing sound? One of the barn cats?

Julia went to investigate. She stepped into the open doorway and looked around. Such a lovely day. The sun had appeared from behind the clouds, bathing the yard and the house in a glowing, golden light. "Anybody here?"

No answer. Nothing seemed to be moving.

As she turned, she heard the creak of hinges. The heavy barn door was crashing toward her. It was too late to move. She felt the impact on the back of her skull. A ferocious pain. The brilliant sunlight faded to black.

Chapter Six

Waiting for Senator Ashbrook, Paul paced the length of the porch and back again. He couldn't stop thinking about Julia's persistent suspicion that General Naylor had been murdered. Her theory about how the general might have been knocked unconscious before he was shot was a possibility. But why was he dressed in his uniform? And how did the killer get into the room without being seen on the surveillance tapes? And the window? It hadn't been forced. Maybe Paul should go upstairs and take another look at that window frame.

Senator Ashbrook emerged from the front doorway and closed it behind him. As he approached, his manner was cordial but reserved. "How can I help you, Deputy?"

Mentally, Paul changed gears, leaving his questions about the general's suicide for another time. "I'm still looking into the vehicular death of John Maser."

A frown appeared on the senator's forehead beneath his gleaming white hair. "The gentleman who hailed from Washington? What about him?"

"He had ties to your home state of Wyoming." Paul took his time in phrasing the next question so it wouldn't sound like an accusation. "John Maser was involved with a survivalist group that calls themselves the Lone Wolves. I hoped you might have information on them."

"As a matter of fact, I do." Ashbrook's frown deepened. "Their leader's name is Henry Wolf, hence their moniker. And they made a significant monetary contribution to my last campaign."

He couldn't believe the senator had admitted to this association. "Are you aware that the Lone Wolves have been in negotiations to purchase high-powered weaponry?"

"No."

His response was unusually emphatic and direct for a slippery politician. Paul followed up. "How much do you know about their activities?"

"Very little."

The senator either didn't mind being linked with survivalist whack balls who were apparently building an arsenal, or he had a clever ulterior motive. Paul suspected the latter. "Why did you tell me about this?"

"Their contribution is a matter of record—something you would discover fairly quickly. I must hasten to add that as soon as my campaign manager discovered that the Lone Wolves were a fringe group with an antigovernment bias, we returned every penny of their money. Here's the truth, Deputy." He made a pointing gesture as though he were addressing a throng. "I'm a card-carrying member of the NRA, and I believe these groups have a right to exist. But I don't support their rhetoric."

"Do you believe the Lone Wolves are dangerous?"

He shrugged. "Probably not. They seem more like a bunch of guys who get together on the weekends to spout conspiracy theory and play soldier."

"I assume you're no longer in contact with them."

"What's their connection with your dead man? Was he a supplier of weaponry?"

It didn't escape Paul's notice that

although Ashbrook was careful to deny knowledge of weapons, he hadn't repudiated all connection to the Lone Wolves. But of course, he wouldn't. Even the members of a fringe survivalist group were Wyoming voters.

"Senator, now that you've had a few days to think about it, are you sure you don't know John Maser?"

He shook his head slowly. The sunlight glinted in his silver hair. "I meet a lot of people in my work, Deputy. The name John Maser doesn't sound familiar."

"I appreciate your time, sir."

Paul went down the stairs from the porch to his Explorer. Julia had been right about one thing. The senator acted like a man who was up to something.

JULIA'S EYELIDS OPENED slowly. She saw nothing but murky gray. Where was she? What had happened to her?

A fierce pain radiated from the back of her head, and she winced. The muscles in her arms and shoulders tensed. She realized that she was curled in a ball. Facedown in a pile of hay.

The barn! She was in the barn. The heavy

door had swung shut, crashing against her skull, knocking her off her feet.

A shrill whinny pierced the air. She lifted her head, looked up and saw Stormy. How had Julia gotten in here? Why was she in Stormy's stall? The pregnant mare pawed the floor, tossed her head.

When Julia moved her arm, Stormy reacted. She reared back on her hind legs. Her hooves came down hard. The floor shook. Julia trembled. If she wasn't careful, she'd be trampled by this nervous mare.

Slowly, she rotated her shoulder and placed her palm on the floor of the stall. She pulled her legs up under her until she was on her knees. Even though her movements were slow and careful, Stormy was spooked, shaking her head and snorting as she rocked back and forth. Her swollen belly swayed. She danced on sharp hooves capable of crushing bone.

The horse reared again.

This time, Julia sprang into action. She bolted to her feet. The sudden movement made her dizzy. Her head throbbed. Her peripheral vision was darkness. The sheer, overwhelming black threatened to overwhelm her.

As Stormy plunged toward her, she dodged clumsily, backed into the corner of the stall.

Julia tried to speak, to whisper reassurance to the horse. Her throat was too tight to squeeze out a single word. Her strength was fading. Her legs were rubber. She braced herself against the stall. "Stormy, hush."

The horse jolted back and forth. Her eyes were wild. She was panicked.

Julia shook her head to clear the cobwebs and was rewarded with a searing pain. Damn it! This shouldn't be happening. Not to her. She was a trained agent.

Her anger brought a surge of adrenaline and gave her the strength she needed. She edged her way around the stall. Reaching through the slats, she unfastened the latch, pushed open the gate and stumbled through. When she'd relatched it, she turned and scanned the barn.

No one else was here.

Gasping, she rested her hand on her breast and felt the heavy thud of her own heartbeat. She could have been killed. If she hadn't gotten out of that stall, Stormy might have trampled her to death.

But this wasn't the horse's fault. Someone had knocked Julia unconscious and dragged her into that stall. Someone wanted her dead.

AFTER SHE GOT Stormy calmed, Julia went into the house and directly to her third-floor bedroom where she locked the door behind her. Would locking up do any good? It hadn't saved the general.

Her suspicions coalesced into dire certainty. General Naylor had been murdered. And the person who killed him was after her.

The assault in the barn had been clever. Julia hadn't seen her attacker. Not even a small glimpse. If she hadn't wakened when she did, her death by trampling would have looked like an accident. Investigators would assume she'd been careless.

Not Paul. He'd know. He'd be smart enough to realize that she knew how to handle horses and would never put herself in a dangerous position. She wished he was here right now, holding her in his big, strong arms and telling her that everything would be okay. *Oh, Paul, I need you.* It seemed like she'd been alone all her life, fighting her own battles. The ache in her head intensified. Her eyelids squeezed shut and a tear slid down her cheek.

Angrily, she rubbed the moisture away. Crying wouldn't do any good. *Pull yourself together. You've got to be strong.* A highly trained FBI agent didn't whine and weep. It was her duty to act—to figure out who killed the general and attacked her, to bring the guilty to justice.

At the same time, she had to protect the sanctity of the safehouse.

She peeled off her clothes, filthy from rolling around in the stall, and slipped into her terry-cloth robe. Taking her gun with her, she went down the hall to the bathroom.

The third floor where she and her staff stayed was a bare bones arrangement. Four small bedrooms and one shared bathroom for herself, Roger Flannery and Craig Lennox.

Should she tell the other two agents what had happened to her? Though Julia was the senior agent and they were supposed to take orders from her, Roger and Craig had ambitions of their own. If she outlined the situation to them, they would very likely report to their superiors. And Julia would have to admit she'd tampered with the crime scene. Her career would be over. The safehouse would be closed down or turned over to someone more competent.

Gingerly, she unfastened her ponytail. When she touched the knot on the back of her head, the result was a shooting pain. But the skin hadn't been broken. No doubt, her thick ponytail saved her from more serious injury.

Inside the medicine cabinet, she found a bottle of aspirin and gulped down three tablets. She'd been unconscious, which meant a slight concussion. Head wounds were tricky; she ought to have it looked at. But what if the doctor wanted to keep her overnight? What if she had to explain how she'd been injured?

No doctors. She sure as hell didn't intend to end her FBI career in a hospital bed like a sad little victim. She was tougher than that.

Gritting her teeth, she turned on the water for a shower. It was usually a little warmer on the third floor than in the rest of the house, but she was burning up. She glanced at the locked bathroom door. It was very little security. Julia was no expert, and she could pick that lock. Did she dare step into the shower? Separated from her gun?

Instead, she switched the water flow to a bath. In the tub, she could keep her weapon nearby and could see the door. She lowered herself into the hot water and scrubbed until her skin was pink. Her energy was returning. And her determination.

She wasn't beaten. Not yet. Julia would find the murderer. And she would maintain the safehouse. But she couldn't do it alone. She needed help. She needed Paul.

THOUGH HE WAS GLAD to get another phone call from Julia, Paul was also worried. There was an intensity in her voice that bothered him, and she was acting mysterious—insisting that she couldn't talk on the phone, had to see him in person.

Of course he'd meet her. At a few minutes after four o'clock in the afternoon, he parked outside the Sundown Tavern in Redding—a local hangout with a bar in the front area. Pool tables were in the back room where nonalcoholic beverages were served. This musty old log building at the edge of the trees had been here as long as Paul could remember, and some of the patrons sitting at the bar under the neon beer signs seemed as deeply rooted as an old growth forest. There was a man with a grizzled, gray beard who always sat by himself, scribbling in a spiral notebook. A couple of construction workers in steel-toed boots. A guy in a battered cowboy hat looked up at the television screen where the Bronco game was winding down to the last quarter.

He spotted Julia, sitting alone at a corner table. In the dim light of the tavern, her healthy complexion seemed as out of place as a blooming red rose in a storage attic. She lifted a coffee mug to her lips and sipped.

He sat opposite her and signaled to the bartender that he also wanted coffee. Technically, Paul was still on duty for another hour.

She started talking. "Paul, I need your help. I know it's unfair for me to ask, but I have nowhere else to turn. I'm putting my career in your hands. Everything I've worked for. My reputation. My years of service. My dreams. Everything."

He didn't feel worthy of such trust. Still, he said, "I'll try not to disappoint you."

"You couldn't," she said. "It's the other

way around. I'm the one who messed up. Big time."

His coffee was served by the burly bartender who knew Paul well enough to add two containers of cream and three packets of real sugar. "What's the score?" Paul asked.

"A blowout. Twenty-six to seven. Broncos."

"Good deal." Life was always better when the home team won. As Paul doctored his thick dark coffee, he said to Julia, "Start at the beginning."

She glanced around nervously, then leaned toward him. Her voice was low, barely more than a whisper, though he was fairly sure nobody could hear them over the television. "When I discovered the general's body, I saw two things that made me think he'd been murdered. As you recall, he wore his Marine Corps dress blues."

Paul would never forget the sight of General Harrison Naylor decked out in his full uniform, lying on his bed with a bullet through his head. "Go on."

"Right away, I knew something was wrong. His shoes were scuffed, and his medals were in the wrong order."

"How would you know about the medals?"

"My brother was a Marine, killed in action three years ago. I was responsible for laying him out in the coffin, and I studied the manual to make sure his medals were correct. Marines are very careful about their uniforms. It's a point of pride. The general never would have dressed himself incorrectly. Somebody else pinned those medals on his chest."

"I remember the general's shoes," he said. "They were freshly polished."

Julia drew a ragged breath. A flush turned her cheeks a bright crimson. "After I found the body, I removed the general's shoes and polished them. And I changed the medals so they would be in the correct order. I tampered with a crime scene."

He was stunned. This confession wasn't what he'd expected. Not from FBI Special Agent Julia Last. "Why?"

"Protecting the safehouse. A murder investigation is intrusive, to say the least. It would have meant the end of Last's Resort."

"To say the least." Anger washed over him as he realized that she'd played him for a fool. He remembered how he'd readily believed the general's death was suicide. Paul had urged the sheriff toward a speedy acceptance of the suicide theory so Julia wouldn't be bothered or upset. "Was there anything else you tampered with?"

"Nothing. I swear."

"So the room was locked. There was no further cleaning up of evidence. The surveillance tapes were correct. You didn't rewrite the suicide note."

"I only touched the medals and the shoes."

"Wearing gloves," he said.

She nodded. "I know better than to leave fingerprints."

His blood began to boil. Harshly, he said, "Very thorough. Nobody will pick up on that clue. You should be proud of yourself."

"Pride is the furthest thing from my mind."

"I've heard it said that former lawmen—and women—make good criminals because they know how to manipulate a crime scene."

"I made a mistake."

"Manipulate," he repeated. "As in jerking me around."

"You're angry," she said.

"Hell, yes." He stared across the table at her. If she hadn't looked so damned miserable, he would have slapped the cuffs on her and marched her out the door. "Why are you telling me this now? You could have gotten away with it. Could have saved your precious safehouse."

"Please listen to me."

So she could tell him more lies? He'd been completely gullible, putty in her hands. His instincts told him to bolt. *Get away from her. Run as fast as you can.*

He could no longer gaze into her beautiful blue eyes and imagine a future with her. Julia was a liar, someone who had committed a criminal act, someone he could never fully trust. He needed to treat her like any other suspect.

"I rationalized at first," she said. "Like you said, it was an impossible crime. I tried to tell myself that I was mistaken, and the general's state of mind was such that he was careless with his uniform."

"Not your call," he said. "The sheriff should have been given full evidence."

"Do you think it's likely the sheriff still would have concluded that the general committed suicide?"

His rising temper made it hard to think straight. "I don't know."

"What about you? Would you have called it suicide?"

"Maybe."

"The facts," Julia said, "didn't change. No one entered or left the general's room. There were no signs of a struggle."

He shot her a stern glare. "That doesn't excuse your actions. You shouldn't have tampered with the scene."

"I know. I can't turn back time and do things differently no matter how much I wish I could." Her lips thinned to a straight line. "The thing I feel worst about is you. I lied to you."

It was more than just a lie. She'd purposely summoned him to the crime scene first. She knew he was sympathetic to her, knew he'd be easy to manipulate. "You used me."

There was a halfhearted cheer from the other patrons in the tavern as the Broncos made another touchdown. A blowout.

She looked down into her coffee mug. Ashamed to look him in the eye? Damn it, he hoped so. He hoped she was hurting half as much as he was.

"I'm sorry, Paul." When she looked up, he saw the shimmer of unshed tears in her eyes. "I have no right to ask you for help."

Her pain and regret reached through his anger and touched him. He didn't want to feel empathy for her. She'd treated him like a chump, and he ought to hate her for that. But he didn't. God help him, he cared about her.

"When I first sat down," he said, "you said you needed something."

"It's wrong to ask you."

"I'm here. And I'm still listening."

She cleared her throat. "I want you to help me catch the general's murderer."

"If there is a murderer," he said. "The facts still point to suicide."

"I know he was killed," she said.

"Why are you so sure?"

"This afternoon, the killer came after me."

Chapter Seven

Back at the safehouse, Julia didn't join the Homeland Security team for dinner. She didn't trust herself to sit across the table from someone who had tried to kill her without betraying her anger and frustration.

In her third-floor bedroom, she stood at the window, looking out. The snow was starting to fall. Flakes as large as popcorn swirled in the lights outside the house. By tomorrow, a pristine white blanket would cover the meadows, mountains and trees. She loved waking up to a fresh snowfall that made the world look clean and beautiful.

Exhaling a sigh, she rubbed at her nape. The throbbing in her head had subsided, replaced by a brand-new kind of pain. Heartache.

She'd disappointed Paul. As she sat across from him in the tavern, she'd watched his dimples disappear. The approving light from his dark brown eyes faded to a cold, angry glare. He would never trust her again.

And yet, he didn't abandon her. When she told him about the attack in the barn, his concern for her physical safety took precedence over his hostility. He had pointed out that she couldn't stay at the safehouse with a murderer on the loose.

Though Julia liked to think she could protect herself, especially when forewarned, she had to agree. This killer had managed to slip into and out of the general's bedroom without being seen. She wasn't safe behind a locked door. If she intended to get any sleep at all tonight, she had to be somewhere else. Paul insisted that she stay with him.

Their plan was for him to pick her up at eight o'clock tonight. She would return to the safehouse at five in the morning.

She looked out at the snowfall. Right now, the storm seemed benign enough, but a blizzard was predicted. The people at the ski lodges would be happy.

At a quarter to eight, she figured the Homeland Security people would be safely tucked away in their meeting room in the basement. She took a small, canvas bag containing her overnight necessities and went downstairs to the kitchen where Roger was still cleaning up the dishes.

"How's the headache?" he asked.

"Much better," she said. "So much better that I'm going out tonight."

He turned away from the sink so quickly that he dripped soapy water on the floor. "On a date?"

"That's right," she said with bravado. "And I probably won't be back until morning."

She expected him to object. They were operating on a round-the-clock schedule, which meant one of the agents needed to be awake and on surveillance duty all night. Instead of grumbling, Roger dried his hands on a dish towel and patted her on the shoulder. "Good for you, Julia."

"You and Craig will have to take my shift tonight."

"Is it that deputy? Paul Hemmings?"

"Yes."

"Excellent. You need to get out."

"Need to?" Her lack of social life was evident to anybody who worked here, but she hadn't thought it was a problem. "What are you suggesting?"

"It's just that I've been here for three months, and I haven't seen you take any time off. Nobody can be an ace FBI agent 24/7. You've got to take some time for, you know, recreation. It'll improve your mood."

It didn't take much reading between the lines to understand what Roger was implying. He thought she needed to get laid. Then she might not be superbitch.

Unfortunately, Julia didn't think sex would be included in her night with Paul. He could barely stand to look at her. "Thanks for understanding, Roger. I'll be back in the morning."

After donning her heavy parka and scarf, she went out on the front porch to wait for Paul. The cold air stung her cheeks. Reaching into her pockets, she pulled out her ski gloves. Though the snowfall was continuous, it wasn't yet heavy. The graded road leading to the safehouse was relatively clear.

"Hey, Julia." David Dillard sauntered from the house. "Pretty night, huh?"

She forced a smile. "David, what are you doing here? I thought you were in session."

"The others are busy with my simulation, and I thought I'd take a break." He removed his black-frame glasses to peer into the dark and snow. "I get restless after being indoors all day."

"Everyone else got a break after lunch." During the time when she was attacked in the barn. "You were busy with your computers in the basement."

"The time was worth it. This simulation is excellent. Even RJ is having trouble figuring out the details on this terrorist attack scenario. The takeover of a nuclear power plant."

"Should you be telling me about this?"

"There's nothing top secret about the big picture. It's got lots of bad guys running around. Several possible escapes and solutions."

"You make it sound like a computer game."

"That's what it is. Only with more accurate detail. Before I joined the FBI, I used to write software gaming programs."

As he shivered inside his heavy-knit sweater, she noticed how skinny he was— the typical computer guy who couldn't be bothered with stopping to eat or to exercise. There were dark circles under his eyes. "Are you taking care of yourself, David? You look tired."

"A little tired," he admitted. "I have trouble getting my brain to shut down so I can go to sleep."

"Insomnia?"

"Yep, and I'm not the only one. I tried one of RJ's sleeping pills last night, but I don't think I'll do that again."

"Why not?"

"They gave me weird dreams. Paranoid stuff."

When she saw Paul's headlights coming up the drive, Julia's heart gave a joyful little leap. This evening might have been a real date. She might have been looking forward to an evening of warmth, friendship and maybe…something more intimate.

"Going out?" David asked.

"Just for the evening."

When she reached for her overnight bag, he had already clasped the handle. "I can carry this for you."

"That won't be necessary." She tugged it away from him. "Good night, David."

"Okay, then. Have fun."

She tromped down the steps. As soon as Paul parked, she went around to the passenger side and yanked open the door. When she looked back at the safehouse, David was waving. Roger had also come out on the porch to watch her departure. Good grief! Their attention made her feel like a teenager on her first date.

She fastened her seat belt before glancing toward Paul. He had no smile for her tonight as he nodded toward the porch. "What's with those guys?"

"I told them this was a date."

"So they're seeing you off," he grumbled. "As if you're not a grown woman."

"I don't go out much." How pathetic! She sounded like an old maid. In a more up-beat tone, she added, "It's the general opinion of the male agents at the house that I should get out more. They think if I had a boyfriend, I'd be easier to live with."

He made no comment as he backed the Explorer around and drove away from the safehouse.

Unlike the other times they'd been together, the silence that spread between them was decidedly uncomfortable. She felt a desperate need to fill the air with words. "It's not true that I *need* a boyfriend. A woman doesn't *need* a man to be happy and fulfilled. I do just fine on my own. By myself."

"I don't believe you."

His comment surprised her. "What?"

"Don't get me wrong. This has nothing to do with whether you're a woman or a man. Everybody's happier when they're in a good relationship. That's a fact."

"A fact, huh? It doesn't sound scientific to me."

"Call it a theory," he said. "Everybody needs somebody. Whether it's their kids, their friends or a special person. It's what we're all looking for."

"Love?"

"Love, approval, sharing, caring. Whatever you want to call it."

"Do you have any proof for this theory?"

He almost grinned. "Late at night, when I look in my daughters' bedroom and see them sleeping like angels, that's my proof. The way I feel about Jennifer and Lily makes my life worth living."

Oh, how she liked this great, big man! The picture he painted was wonderfully simple and complete. But the deep love he had for his children was far different than a relationship between a man and a woman. "Is that how you felt about your ex-wife?"

"Not all the time. That's for damn sure.

Remember, I said a *good* relationship. You know what I mean."

Actually, she did know. At age thirty-two, Julia had done her share of thinking about whether her future included marriage and family. Her career was great, but she wanted children. And a home. And a partner—a man who would become an inseparable part of her life. "A good relationship is hard work."

"Seems to me it's just a matter of finding the right person."

"How? There are millions of people on the planet. How do you find the right one? It's like panning for gold. You sit by the creek, sifting through a million grains of sand and never find the one tiny particle that sparkles. And if you do? Half the time, it turns out to be pyrite. Fool's gold."

"You're cynical," he said.

"I call it practical."

"Whatever." He shrugged. "We need to make a stop at the skating rink. Lily forgot her bag last night, and I need to pick it up."

Surreptitiously, she watched him as he concentrated on the road where the conditions were worsening by the moment. Not only was he good-hearted and kind, but Paul was a fine-looking man—big, strong and masculine. Especially big. He was so tall that the crown of his head almost touched the roof of the SUV. His gloved hands on the steering wheel were huge.

When she was growing up, she had reached her full height by the time she was twelve. Her brother had joked that it would take a big man to handle her. Like Paul? Was he everything she'd been looking for? Had she stumbled across a solid gold future?

When he parked at the door outside the skating rink, she noticed there were no other cars in the lot. "It doesn't look open."

"It's not. But I have a key. Sometimes, when the coach can't make it, I'll open up early for practice."

"Do you coach, too?"

"Not figure skating," he said. "I help out with hockey on occasion."

She followed him inside. When he turned on the lights, the big empty building echoed like the inside of a cavern. She was drawn toward the huge mirror of ice. "It's been a while since I've gone skating. I used to be pretty good."

"Figure skating?" he called out as he

went toward the counter where ice skates were rented.

"I've been known to do a couple of spins," she said. "But I really like to go fast."

"Me, too." He waved a pink gym bag. "Found it."

She stood at the edge of the rink, gazing wistfully at the smooth surface. Back home in Wisconsin, she and her brother had skated on the frozen pond at the edge of town. The first skate of the winter was always the most dangerous because the ice might crack and you'd be dumped in the freezing water. She remembered a time when it snapped under their feet. They both came to a halt, afraid to move a muscle. Cautiously, they dropped to their knees and crawled across the frozen surface—scared to death and laughing at the same time. She missed her brother's laughter most of all.

Paul came up beside her. He held out a pair of well-worn white ice skates. "I brought you a size ten. Is that right?"

"Good guess."

"Put them on and show me your stuff, Julia."

Though he wasn't smiling, this was a

friendly gesture. A step toward reconcilia-
tion. "You're skating, too. Right?"

"You bet."

As PAUL JAMMED his foot into his own skate,
he told himself that he was making a big
mistake. It wasn't smart to forgive Julia.
She'd lied to him, manipulated him and used
him.

When she first told him about tampering
with the crime scene, he should have turned
her over to the sheriff and walked away fast.
Breaking the rules wasn't his thing, especially not in the case of a suspicious death
that might be murder.

But he couldn't desert her. Whether or not
it made good sense, he cared about this
woman. And when she told him she'd been
attacked, he had to protect her.

But he was done playing the fool. After
they left the rink and went to his house, after
the kids were in bed, he intended to sit her
down and make her understand what they
had to do. This investigation should be
turned over to the proper authorities even
though she might be in a lot of trouble and
it meant the end of her safehouse operation.

"I'm ready," she said as she peeled off

her parka. Standing firmly on her skates, her smile was bright and warm enough to melt the ice. Wisps of curly brown hair had escaped her ponytail and framed her face. Her blue eyes shimmered.

If the safehouse closed down, she'd leave the area and go on to her next FBI assignment. He was damn sure he'd never see her again. *That hurt. He didn't want to lose her.*

With sure strokes, she glided across the smooth white surface. Her blue sweater outlined her hourglass figure. She was great to look at. Not like those skinny little girls that twirled like twigs in a storm. Julia's breasts thrust forward. Her movements were strong and steady, more like a speed skater than a figure skating twinkletoes. Her hips rotated from side to side. When she reached the far end of the rink, she crossed one leg in front of the other to make the turn. Nice move.

He plowed across the ice with little grace and a lot of muscle, slowing to round the curves and picking up speed on the straightaway. The exercise felt good, stretching his muscles after sitting too long in the car. He circled the rink. He was flying. His heart beat faster.

When he looked over, Julia was right beside him. She was doing a good job of keeping up with him, matching him stride for stride.

At the curve, she slipped and let out a yelp, almost falling. He reached over and placed an arm around her waist. It seemed natural when she snuggled against him.

He knew he was making a mistake when he pulled her close, but he couldn't resist. Without even trying, they skated in tandem. A perfect fit.

Though there wasn't any music, they moved to a synchronized beat, knowing each other's rhythm. It was almost like dancing, especially when she turned in his arms so they were face-to-face with Julia skating backward.

"Show off," he teased.

"You try it."

They switched positions, and he glided toward the center of the ice where they spun in a slippery circle and came to a stop.

Julia was breathing hard. She held both his hands in her own. "Let's stay here all night. Let's forget about everything else and just skate."

As he gazed down into her face, he

wished that life could be that simple. But it wasn't. They both had responsibilities. Not to mention a possible murder to solve. "We need to get going."

"Once more around the rink. Please."

Before he could reply, the lights went out. They were standing in the middle of the rink in pitch darkness.

"Hey," Paul yelled. "Who's there?"

Julia released her grasp on his hands. "I don't like this," she said.

"It's somebody playing a joke."

"If not," she said quietly, "I'm drawing my weapon."

"You have a gun?"

"I'm always armed."

Any illusion he might have had about Julia being sweet and defenseless was gone. He unholstered his own gun and shouted again, "Turn on the lights."

He felt her tug on his sleeve. "We should get off the ice," she said. "We make an easy target here."

"You're right." He tried to orient himself using the faint glow from the few windows in the rink. But he wasn't sure which way they were heading. Toward the exit? Toward the dressing rooms?

He could barely see Julia beside him. She slipped. He heard her fall with a thud and a soft curse.

When he tried to help her up, his feet went out from under him. He sprawled. The cold ice surface bit into his hands. Side by side, they crawled toward the waist-high guardrail. They moved fast. No time for nonsense.

"I'm at the edge," Julia said quietly. "I'm climbing over."

"Right behind you." He grabbed the rail and pulled himself to his feet.

The lights came on. The sudden burst of illumination blinded him. After an instant of disorientation, Paul went into a crouch and aimed his weapon toward the front door where the light switches were. Behind the guardrail, Julia did the same.

He saw a figure in a black ski mask. He had a gun of his own. This wasn't a joke.

"Police," Paul shouted.

The figure took a few steps toward the ice.

"Throw down your weapon," Paul shouted. "Do it. Now."

Instead, the dark figure pivoted and ran toward the exit. He was getting away, and there wasn't a damn thing Paul could do to give chase. Not on ice skates.

From across the arena, he heard the door of the skating rink slam. Their would-be assassin was gone.

"I guess we scared him off," Julia said as she stood behind the wall.

"He had a gun."

"So do we."

And they were a formidable twosome. Though Paul should have been thinking about filing reports and alerting the sheriff to this incident, the rush of adrenaline was exciting. He was proud of Julia and of himself.

They'd been threatened. And they had won.

Next time, it might not be so easy.

Chapter Eight

Julia tore off her ice skates and followed Paul across the arena to the entrance. Still holding her gun at the ready, she positioned herself as tactical backup as he whipped the door open.

The wet, cold air blasted into the arena, momentarily blinding her. Bracing her gun in both hands, she stepped up beside Paul. The heavy snowfall and blowing wind had already begun to erase the footprints of their would-be assassin. Though it had been only minutes since he left the arena, he was out of reach. His taillights vanished in the storm. The tire prints were nearly obliterated.

"Too much snow," Paul said as he pulled the door closed. "There's nothing out there we can use as a clue."

Compared to the storm raging outside,

the arena was utterly silent. Julia allowed her gun hand to drop to her side. She scanned the area where they were standing. The man in the black ski mask had worn gloves, which meant there would be no fingerprints. And he didn't fire his weapon. So there would be no shells or bullets that could be used in ballistic analysis.

If she hadn't experienced that instant of panic when the lights went out, she might not have believed they'd been threatened. "Any idea of his identity?"

He shook his head. "In Eagle County, the usual suspects don't include armed assassins in ski masks. Our local troublemakers are drunks, druggies and guys with bad tempers. Not professional criminals."

"You're assuming the man in the ski mask was a hired gun?"

"A hit man."

She had to agree. The Homeland Security people at the safehouse were in a meeting, and none of them would have taken this kind of risk. Instead, they'd hired someone else to do their dirty work. "Not a very effective hit man. As soon as he saw we were armed, he retreated."

"A wise move," he said. "When he turned

the lights back on, he probably expected to find us floundering around on the ice. Easy targets."

"But we were ready." She and Paul had been side by side with weapons aimed. It had been a very satisfying moment. "Armed and dangerous."

"He must have followed us from the house." Paul glided his hands up and down her arms as if reassuring himself that she was unharmed. "Are you okay?"

"Fine." Her heartbeat was accelerated, and she had the hyperawareness that came from being threatened.

"You know he was here to kill you, Julia."

That realization bothered her far less than the fact that Paul had been with her. She'd dragged him into this web of danger. The hit man would never have allowed Paul to escape unharmed. He was a witness. He could have been shot, and it would have been her fault.

"If you want to call in the sheriff," she said, "I'll understand."

"What's the point? We've got no evidence. There's not a damn thing the forensic people can investigate."

"I was thinking about protection."

"For me?"

"He would have killed you, too." An even worse possibility presented itself in her mind. "What if we hadn't stopped at the skating rink? What if we'd gone directly to your house?"

They might have unwittingly pointed a professional killer toward his home. His children. Oh God, his children! Danger to herself was nothing. It was part of being a federal agent, part of the job. But her actions were responsible for putting innocent children in harm's way.

When she remembered that beautiful little black-haired child spinning on the ice, pure dread coiled tightly around her heart. No horror was more intense than a child in jeopardy. Julia hated herself for what she had brought upon this family. "You've got to take me back to the safehouse."

"Now that I know you're being stalked, there's no way I'm going to leave you."

"That hit man could have come to your house. He could have—"

"It didn't happen," he said.

"I was wrong to ask for your help. I wasn't thinking about anything but my own needs." Her decision to approach him might have resulted in unthinkable tragedy. How could she have been so blind to the possible consequences? To endanger his children? "I'm so sorry."

"I know."

At the ragged edge of emotional restraint, her breath came in gasps. Her gaze met his, and she searched the depths of his eyes for a sign. He had every reason to hate her. "Can you ever forgive me?"

Gently, he pulled her into his arms. "I can try."

That was the best she could hope for. She trembled against him, needing his solace and comfort.

His voice was quiet. "The important thing now is to figure out what we do next."

In spite of the threat, Paul's mind was clear. His two girls might be in danger. He needed to make the right decisions.

The first thing was to make sure they were protected and safe. If guarding his children meant sitting on his front porch with a shotgun across his lap, that was what he'd do. Gladly. But he couldn't desert Julia. She was in the direct line of fire.

"I can contact the sheriff and demand protective custody." He thought about the guys he worked with. They were a small staff. The sheriff couldn't spare even one deputy to stay at his house night and day.

Julia shivered in his arms. "I never should have touched the general's body."

"You made a mistake." He wasn't about to let her off the hook for that. "I don't know if the evidence you tampered with would have made a difference. It's still an impossible crime. The general's death still looks like suicide."

"Then why is a hit man coming after me?"

He thought for a moment. "Because you're a trained agent on the inside. Frankly, you're the only person who could hope to figure this out."

"Me?" He felt her shaking her head. "I'm not that good. Not a forensic investigator."

"But you know these people." The picture was becoming clear to him. "If there had been a full-scale murder investigation, your four guests would have thrown up all kinds of barriers. Think of the senator. He wouldn't sit still for an interrogation. And the other three are high-ranking people in the FBI and CIA. Their agencies would have closed ranks to protect them."

"What are you saying?"

"We don't have evidence, facts and clues. The only way this killer will be caught is by someone on the inside, someone who can talk to these people, get them to open up."

"Like me?"

"Exactly like you."

Paul knew what had to be done. He gave Julia a squeeze and pulled away from her. "First, I make sure there's no danger to my kids."

Her face was pale, stricken. "How?"

"Mac and Abby are still in town."

He took the cell phone from his pocket. His good buddy Mac was a Denver cop and an expert marksman. Abby was a trained federal agent with several years of undercover work under her belt. They were the perfect twosome for keeping his girls safe. "Mac owes me a big favor. And this is the payoff. He's going to be watching my kids until we have this sorted out."

"And what are you going to do?"

"I'm going back to the safehouse with you."

"Why?"

"Because we're going to solve this murder. You and me, Julia. Together."

IT WAS JUST after nine o'clock when Julia followed Paul up the snow-covered sidewalk outside his house. Apparently, the kids were still awake; lights shone from nearly every window in the two-story clapboard house.

On the porch, he turned to her. "We're not going to talk about any of this in front of the kids."

She nodded. After her emotional turbulence at the rink, she felt drained, exhausted.

"With Mac and Abby keeping watch, the girls will be safe. And there's no reason to start them worrying about me. They've already lost one parent."

"Your ex-wife doesn't stay in touch?"

"Not often enough." He frowned. "Anyway, not a word."

"Understood."

As soon as Paul opened the door, the two little girls raced toward him for hugs. The older girl, Jennifer, wore a long flannel nightie with bunny slippers. The seven-year-old, Lily, had on purple pajamas with a fairy princess on the front.

Paul lifted them off the floor, holding one girl in each arm. "I thought you two would be in bed. Tomorrow's a school day."

"Uncle Jess said we could stay up."

Julia glanced toward the man who sat on the plaid sofa in front of the television. She knew that Jess Isler was a good friend of both Paul and Mac. But she'd never actually met him. He came toward her with his hand outstretched. "You must be Julia."

"And you're Jess." With his streaked blond hair and twinkly blue eyes, he was too pretty for her taste. "How's your recovery going?"

"Very well, thanks." After he released her hand, he went to the front window, pushed the curtain aside and peered out at the snowfall. "Next week, I get to start skiing again."

The older of Paul's daughters wriggled out of his arms. Mimicking Jess's move, she held out her small hand toward Julia. "I'm very pleased to meet you."

"Same here," Julia said. The child was adorable. "I saw you skate last night. You were good."

"And me?" Lily hopped out of her father's arms and braced her fists on her hips. "What about me? I didn't fall down once."

"I'm sure you're fantastic."

"However," Paul said gruffly, "you forgot your gym bag at the rink."

He held it up the pink bag, and Lily snatched it away from him. "Thank you, Daddy." She whipped it open, reached inside and pulled out a half-eaten candy bar.

Before she could take a bite, Paul said, "Freeze."

Lily went completely still. So did Jennifer.

Paul lifted the candy bar from Lily's fingers. "Not right before bed."

Lily groaned.

"No moving," he said. "You know the rules. When I say 'freeze,' you don't move until I say… okay, unfreeze."

"Please," Lily whined. "I'm starving to death."

"We had dinner," Jennifer said. Her dark brown eyes—the same color as her father's—studied Julia. "Do you like to cook, Julia?"

"Very much. And I especially like to bake. Breads and cookies."

"Would you show me how?"

"I'd love to. Nothing smells as good as baking bread."

As Julia took off her parka and boots, Jess came over beside Paul. "The sheriff called. He wanted you to call him back at home as soon as you got in."

"Wonder why he didn't use my cell

phone." Paul shrugged and turned to the girls. "I need to take care of this business, and you two kids need to be in bed."

"We can stay up," Jennifer said. "There's not going to be school tomorrow. It's a blizzard."

"You wish," he said. "I want those teeth brushed and faces washed."

Jennifer latched on to Julia's hand. "Come with me."

Lily took her other hand. "And me."

As they marched up the staircase to the second floor, the girls chatted about how school would for sure be canceled tomorrow.

Inside the bathroom, Lily tugged on Julia's hand and motioned for her to come close. When she leaned down, Lily asked, "Are you Daddy's girlfriend?"

"We're friends."

"I think he likes you," Lily said. "You're big like him."

"Jeez, Lily." Jennifer rolled her eyes. "She didn't mean that you look like a man."

"I didn't say that. I think she's pretty."

Julia cut in. "Aren't you two supposed to be brushing your teeth?"

The girls took turns at the sink. More than

once, Lily caught Julia's eye in the mirror and smiled sweetly. It was becoming obvious that these two young ladies wanted another female in the house; they missed having a mother.

Lily led the way down the hall to their bedroom. "It's the master bedroom," she said. "Because there's two of us and only one of Daddy."

Their room was an explosion of pink with white four-posters on opposite sides of the large room and lots of shelves for a play area in the middle. Herds of stuffed animals lurked in the corners.

Lily hopped up on her bed. "Tell me a story."

"Do you have a book you'd like to read?"

"Make up a story. About a princess."

Jennifer said, "You don't have to if you don't want to."

"Not a problem," Julia said. "Let's all sit over here on Lily's bed, and I'll tell you a story about skaters. Have you ever heard of Hans Brinker?"

"Never," Jennifer said. "Is he a famous ice skater like Timothy Goebel? He does quads. I love him."

With one girl on either side, Julia started

to tell the story she only vaguely recalled. "Hans Brinker was from Holland and his family was very poor…"

She invented most of the details about a contest to win a pair of beautiful silver ice skates and how much Hans wanted those skates. Then came the part about sticking his finger in the dike and staying there all night long.

"Wait a minute," Lily said. "Did he miss the contest?"

Julia wasn't sure, but she decided this story would have a happy ending. Hans was a hero. He saved his little town. "Even though he was really tired from staying at the dike all night long, he won the contest the next day. And he had his silver skates."

"Is this a true story?" Jennifer asked.

"It's a legend. Maybe true. Maybe not. The important thing is that Hans did the right thing even though it was really hard."

She looked up and saw Paul standing in the doorway. He smiled with infinite gentleness. His dimples appeared and softened his rugged features. The glow from his dark eyes showed pure affection. He adored these children. As he'd told her earlier this evening, the girls were what made his life worth living, and she was honored to be a part of this family if only for a moment.

When Paul joined her to tuck the girls under their comforters, she savored the special warmth that surrounded them—the warmth that came from unconditional love.

Before Paul left the bedroom, he switched off the overhead light. "Sleep tight, girls. I need to go out tonight for work, and I might not be back in the morning. But Mac and Abby are coming over to stay with you."

"Okay," Lily said. "Daddy?"

"What is it, honey?"

"Is Julia your girlfriend?"

"She's a friend and a girl." He tossed a grin over his shoulder toward Julia, then looked back at his children. "I guess that makes her a girl friend."

"I like her," Jennifer said.

"Me, too," Lily piped up.

"Good night." Paul eased the door closed. "I love you both."

"Love you back."

Though the children weren't asleep and there was no particular need to be quiet, Julia tiptoed down the hallway. She didn't want to risk disturbing this unexpected aura of family and belonging. His children liked her. They accepted her and thought she was a good match for their father. Because she was, as Lily pointed out, a big woman. Julia grinned to herself. Never before had the breadth of her shoulders counted as a virtue.

In the living room, Paul went to a worn armchair—similar in style to some of the heavy furniture at the safehouse. He sat and leaned back. His eyes closed. He rubbed at his forehead.

She sat on the sofa. Jess was nowhere in sight.

When Paul looked over at her, she couldn't tell what he was thinking. He had so many faces. With the girls, he was a good father. On the job, he was a hard-working deputy. At the ice-skating rink, he had been her protector. Could he ever be her lover? Was that expression in his repertoire?

She wanted to be Paul's girlfriend—a real girlfriend with commitment and relationship. But so much negativity had passed between them. She'd betrayed him. She'd brought danger to his family.

Telling him that she was sorry wasn't enough to regain his trust. She knew that.

"That phone call from the sheriff," he said. "It was about the preliminary autopsy results."

Though solving the possible murder of the general should have been her number-one priority, she didn't want to think about crime. She'd rather stay here in this cozy house with the comfortable clutter of children's toys. Still, Julia asked, "What did they find?"

"The general had no external injuries that might suggest he was knocked unconscious. The cause of his death was gunshot wound to the head." He exhaled a heavy sigh. "No evidence points to murder. The medical examiner believes this was suicide."

"But you and I know that's wrong. If the general wasn't murdered, no one would be coming after me."

"There were two autopsies done. One on the general. The other on John Maser."

"The victim from the car accident."

"It wasn't careless driving that made him go off the road," Paul said. "The tox screen showed a high level of morphine in his system but no indication that he was a user. On his left arm, there was a hypodermic puncture wound. He was shot full of drugs and turned loose on a dangerous mountain road."

"Murdered," she said.

"The sheriff wants me to do further interrogation on the people staying at your safehouse. That gives me a reason to stay there."

She wished the reason was because he wanted to be with her. *Everybody needs somebody.*

Chapter Nine

The snowstorm continued unabated. Road conditions were miserable, but Paul had driven in worse. He eased his four-wheel drive SUV along the road at a slow, steady speed to avoid going into a skid. His windshield wipers whipped back and forth. Visibility through the swirling snow was almost nil. "Jennifer might have been right. This could be a blizzard."

"It's good for the skiers," Julia said.

"For them, it's perfect."

And for Paul? Extreme weather was never good news for the sheriff's department. There were always emergencies. Lost cross-country skiers. Car accidents. Power outages.

This time, however, these problems weren't his responsibility. The sheriff had ordered him to investigate the possible connection between the morphine-related death of John Maser and the four remaining guests at Julia's lodge. Not an easy task.

He carefully negotiated the turn onto the road leading to the safehouse. Within an hour, these back roads would be impassable. It was lucky that Mac and Abby had gotten to his house when they did. Paul had no qualms about leaving his daughters in their care.

"You're going to be snowed in at the safehouse," Julia said.

"I expect so."

"It's no problem. We have available bedrooms on the second and third floor. You'd probably prefer the second floor. You only have to share a bathroom with one other person and—"

"I'm staying in your room, Julia."

"Oh."

Though the car heater blasted on high, there was a chill in the car. He'd avoided thinking about what might happen if they shared a bedroom. Making love to Julia was a strong temptation. He couldn't deny that he'd been imagining what it would be like to hold her strong, sexy body in his arms and to kiss her sweet pink lips. But he couldn't forget that she'd used him, played on his gullibility and dragged him into a threatening situation. If he made love to her, he'd be an even bigger fool than he was before.

"We can't stay in the same room," she said. "I'm the senior agent at the safehouse. It sets a bad example if I have a guest of the opposite sex in my bedroom."

If he'd dared to take his eyes off the road, he would have glared at her. They had a murderer on the loose. And a hit man who came after them at the rink. This was no time to worry about her reputation. "I'm staying in your room," he repeated. "I can't protect you if I'm sleeping down the hall."

"I can protect myself."

"Not this time. We have a killer who walks through locked doors."

"Of course, he doesn't, but—"

"The main reason I'm coming back here with you is to keep you safe. Which means I'm staying in your room."

She exhaled a prolonged sigh. "I guess you're right."

"You're supposed to be my girlfriend," he reminded her. "If our cover story is going to work, you'll need to pretend that you're glad to have me in your bed."

"I can do that."

He was surprised to hear a smile in her voice. "I'm not expecting an Academy Award performance."

"That's good because I'm not talented enough to do convincing undercover work. But I can act like your girlfriend. I'll give you little hugs and kisses on the cheek." Her gloved hand rested on his shoulder. "This might be the best assignment I've ever had."

"Being my girlfriend?"

"Having you in my bedroom."

Snow drifts completely covered the road ahead of them. There weren't any other tire tracks to follow. Paul squinted through the windshield, through the curtain of falling snow. "Did you just say that you want to go to bed with me?"

"You heard me."

His fingers tightened on the steering wheel. This was one hell of a way to find out that she was as interested in sex as he was. Paul wasn't sure how to deal with this information. So much had changed since he'd first seen Julia chopping wood and had thought she was the perfect woman.

Gruffly, he said, "Tell me about the surveillance system at the safehouse."

"You already know about the exterior cameras protecting the perimeter and the cameras in the hallways." Her hand withdrew from his shoulder. Her tone became crisp and businesslike. "We also have interior cameras focused on the front door and kitchen door. The lower level where we have our office isn't monitored."

"That's the area you kept secret when the sheriff and paramedics were picking up the general's body."

"Right."

"What else?" he asked.

"On occasion, with some of our more infamous protected witnesses, we've used listening devices in their bedrooms. All the phones are, of course, bugged."

"So I can assume that somebody might be listening or watching all the time."

"I'll make sure my bedroom is clear," she said. "The rest of the time, we need to be careful about what we say."

"What about your other two agents? Roger and Craig."

"What about them?"

"As far as I'm concerned, they're suspects in the general's murder. They know their way around the safehouse better than your guests.

One of them could have tampered with the surveillance camera outside the general's room."

"Not possible," she said firmly.

"How much do we tell them?"

Again, she sighed. "We'll have to admit that you know about the safehouse. And you're investigating John Maser's murder. We won't mention the general."

"Sounds good to me."

The lights of the safehouse flickered before them. In the midst of the raging storm, the lodge looked like a warm, peaceful sanctuary. It was hard to believe a killer lurked inside.

As Paul slowed, his tires went into a skid, which he managed skillfully as he parked. "Nobody else will be leaving here tonight."

They fought their way through the storm to the front door. When they stepped inside, Roger Flannery greeted them. "What are you two doing back here?"

"You were waiting up for me," Julia accused. "Honestly, Roger. I'm not a teenager on a first date."

"That's a negative on waiting up," he said. "We saw your headlights approaching."

Of course. Roger and Craig would have

been watching the monitors, doing their job. She was the one disobeying the rules and acting irresponsibly. Her blatant disregard for her duties bothered her a great deal. Until now, she'd been an exemplary agent.

Before removing her parka, she asked, "Have you tended to the horses?" she asked.

Roger gave a nod. "They're all bedded down for the night. I tried to clear a path to the barn, but the snow kept drifting. It's bad out there."

"A blizzard," Julia said. "We're going to be snowed in. That's why I came back. If I didn't return tonight, I knew I'd be gone for a while."

Paul stepped forward. "There's no way I can drive back to my house. Looks like you're stuck with me."

Roger's mouth twitched nervously. His eyes darted toward Julia as he said, "Welcome, Paul."

When she saw the look of doubt painted on Roger's face, Julia got a sinking feeling in the pit of her stomach. The first lesson she drilled into the agents who worked at the safehouse was keeping their mission secret. Now she was about to break her own rule. She confronted Roger directly. "Deputy Hemmings knows we're an FBI safehouse."

"He does?"

"In addition to being my friend," Julia said, reminding herself to give Paul a flirtatious little pat on the arm, "the deputy has official business. He's investigating the death of that car-accident victim."

"Who?"

"John Maser," Paul said. "He's from Washington, D.C.—like all your guests."

"It's a big city," Roger said defensively. "None of them had a connection with him, did they?"

"Nothing they'd admit. The sheriff was willing to let it drop. But we have new information. I'm going to need more detailed alibis from your guests."

"Good luck," Roger muttered.

Julia asked, "Are they done with their meeting?"

"Not yet. They took a break about a half hour ago, came upstairs and scarfed down half the cookies I made for tomorrow's dessert." He looked pained at this blatant disregard for his well-planned menu. "Then they went back into session."

She checked her wristwatch. It was half past ten o'clock. "Did they say how long they'd be working?"

"Not to me."

She gave him a nod. "The deputy and I will be going upstairs. Would you please tell Craig that I'll take the three a.m. surveillance shift?"

"Okay." Tight-lipped, he shot a glance at Julia, then at Paul. It was obvious that Roger wasn't sure how to react to the news that his by-the-rules boss intended to spend the night with an outsider.

There was no justification for her behavior. No excuse that wouldn't sound lame. Julia could see her career slipping away, inch by inch. Maybe Roger would be the next senior agent to run this safehouse. Linking her arm with Paul's, she gave him a little wave. "G'night."

With a shrug, he turned back toward the kitchen.

After Julia and Paul hung their wet parkas on pegs near the door, she led him up the staircase past the second floor to the third, then down the hall and into her bedroom, where she shut the door behind them.

The small space was hardly bigger than a monk's cell. She glanced at Paul. The top of his head was less than a foot away from the ceiling. His shoulders seemed cramped. He couldn't take a full stride because most of the floor space was taken up by her full-size bed.

The bed! Oh yes, that was another problem. The bed was barely big enough for her. If Paul stretched out full length on that mattress, his feet would dangle over the end. There was absolutely no way the two of them could lie on that bed without touching.

As she watched him edge around the foot of her bed, she could tell that he was thinking the same thing. One small bed. Two tall people. Not a good fit.

"Perhaps," she said, "we should move downstairs to the empty bedroom. It's bigger."

"Bigger bed?"

"Not really."

"On the second floor," he said, "we're one step closer to the murderer."

Feeling trapped and uncomfortable, she dropped her overnight case on the floor beside her tiny desk and peered out the window. A fierce blast of wind hurled snow against the pane. This should have been a good night to curl up in bed, pull the covers over her head and sleep until the storm passed.

"We're not all that much safer in this room," she said. "It's just up one flight of stairs."

"Fine. Let's check out that bigger room."

They descended the staircase to the second-floor landing where there were six bedrooms. Julia used her set of master keys to open the door to the unoccupied room. "This room shares a bathroom with Gil Bradley. There are locks on either side."

Though the bed was no larger, the floor space was almost double her room. In one corner, a cornflower blue armchair and ottoman were arranged beside a brass standing lamp for reading.

Paul strode across the floor to the bathroom, unfastened the lock and went inside.

When she followed, she saw him standing in front of the open medicine cabinet. The shelves were lined with plastic bottles. Paul picked one up and read the label. "Enchinacea and goldenseal." He picked up another. "Garlic pills. And here's vitamin C, E and B12."

"Gil's a health nut."

"I wonder how he feels about drugs."

"Like morphine?" She wouldn't be a bit surprised if Gil had access to all kinds of substances—legal and illegal. He was the kind of agent who worked on the shadowy fringes, which meant he was also smart enough to be careful. "I hardly think he'd leave his hypodermic kit lying around."

Paul went to the door that opened to Gil's bedroom.

"What are you doing?" she asked.

"I want to search these rooms, and I'm pretty sure our suspects aren't going to give permission." The door handle turned easily in his hand, and he grinned. "Let's see what Gil might be hiding."

"What are we looking for?"

"Anything suspicious."

They didn't have to look far. In Gil's bottom dresser drawer was an automatic handgun and ammunition. Under the bed, they found a leather case with a repeating rifle and a night scope, useful for a sniper.

Gil Bradley was a dangerous man, and these sophisticated weapons reminded her just how scary he was. Apprehension tickled the hairs on the back of her neck. "Maybe he brought the rifle for hunting."

"Not a .50-caliber rifle. Not unless he's going after rhino."

In the back of his closet was a small,

locked suitcase. "He could have anything in there," Paul said.

"Don't even try to open it," she advised. "He's CIA. It'll probably explode if tampered with."

"It's one of those combination locks. You think he'd use 007?"

The longer they stayed in Gil's room, the more her tension increased. "Let's get out of here."

Paul replaced the suitcase in the closet and followed her toward the bathroom. "This is a nice room. And that's a queen-size bed."

"I can't ask Gil to move." Standing inside the bathroom, she motioned for him to hurry. "Come on, Paul."

The door to the bedroom crashed open. Gil Bradley charged inside. Moving at top speed, he was a dangerous blur in Julia's vision. His arms rotated like a windmill as he thrust at Paul's throat with an open hand.

The shock of this unexpected attack left her paralyzed. All the terrifying stories she'd heard about CIA assassins coalesced into one second. Trained killers. With one swift blow, they could kill, blind or permanently disable their opponents.

Paul defended himself with surprising

skill. After he dodged the first assault, he caught hold of Gil's arm near the elbow and used his forward momentum to throw him off balance. The muscular CIA agent recovered and immediately went into an attack stance.

"Hold it," Paul said as he backed away. "I'm on your side."

"What the hell are you doing in here?" Gil's voice was low and seething.

"I can explain." Julia broke through her shock to rush forward. "We're snowed in. Deputy Hemmings and I were looking at the unoccupied bedroom next door."

"You're in my damn room."

He looked angry enough to kill them both, tear them limb from limb and sauté their remains for dinner.

"It's all about the size of the bed," she said desperately. "We were checking out your bed."

The senator appeared in the doorway. "Is there a problem?"

Gil aimed a ferocious glare in his direction. "Nothing I can't handle."

"Julia," Senator Ashbrook snapped in his most officious tone, "why is the deputy here?"

"Glad you asked," Paul said as he wisely moved away from Gil's striking range. "I'm here because I'm investigating the murder of John Maser."

"Murder?" Ashbrook's eyebrows pulled into a scowl. "I thought that was a car accident."

"Get out of my room," Gil said. "All of you."

They moved onto the landing where RJ Katz and David Dillard were standing. Gil whipped the door to his room closed with a sharp click.

"Good," Paul said. "I'm glad you're all together so I only have to say this once. We have new evidence on the death of John Maser that indicates foul play. I need to ask you further questions."

"I don't believe this." RJ Katz widened her eyes. "Are you saying we're suspects?"

"A suspect?" Ashbrook echoed. "Outrageous! I refuse to answer any questions without my lawyer present."

"Same here," RJ said. "Frankly, Julia, you should know better. I'm appalled that you've put us in this position."

Even the mild-mannered David Dillard complained. "It's been a long day. Can't this wait until morning?"

"I can wait," Paul said. "We're snowed in tonight. Nobody's going anywhere."

Julia backed him up. "A very good plan. I suggest we all go to bed and start fresh tomorrow. Sorry for the disturbance. Good night."

RJ turned on her heel. Her slim hips twitched back and forth as she went into her room and slammed the door. The senator matched her huffiness. More calmly, David said good-night.

Julia and Paul stood on the landing with Gil Bradley. His square jaw clenched with barely suppressed rage. Unlike RJ and the senator, Gil would never call on lawyers to protect him.

He looked Paul in the eye. "Let's talk."

Chapter Ten

The smallest room on the first floor of the safehouse was a library with several shelves of well-worn books and a couple of comfortable looking armchairs. In the center of the room was a square table and four sturdy wooden chairs that looked like they'd been stolen from a high school. A huge dictionary lay open on a lectern beneath the window. It wasn't the most comfortable room in the house but one of the most private—a good place for Paul and Julia to have a talk with Gil Bradley.

When Paul lowered himself into one of the hard wooden chairs and stretched his long legs out in front of him, he realized how tired he was. It had been a hell of a long, stressful day. His limbs felt heavy, weighted down with exhaustion. And his forearm ached where he'd blocked the jab that Gil had aimed at his Adam's apple. If that blow had connected, Paul's windpipe might have been crushed. He looked across the table at the former Navy SEAL.

In spite of the fact that Gil was the one who said he wanted to talk, words weren't pouring through his tight lips. He leaned forward in his chair, elbows resting on the tabletop in front of him, tense from head to toe. Cold intelligence gleamed through his squinted eyes.

Paul spoke first. "John Maser. You knew him."

"A jerk," Gil said. "A wannabe mercenary who didn't have the guts to pull it off."

"He was convicted of fraud," Paul pointed out. "So he must have done something."

"Lying. He was good at that."

"What about weapon smuggling? We have information indicating he was involved with the Lone Wolf survivalists."

Gil gave a snort. "Smuggling weapons to Wyoming? That's like smuggling milk to Wisconsin."

"Hey," Julia interrupted. "I'm from Wisconsin. Let's not pick on my home state."

Her attempt to lighten the mood fell flat. Paul was too tired to respond, and Gil had no sense of humor.

"My point," Gil said, "is that guns—even high-powered weapons—are relatively easy to come by in Wyoming. It's a hunting state."

Paul cut to the chase. "Was Maser coming here to see you?"

"No way. I met with Maser about three years ago, decided he was a poseur and didn't want anything more to do with him. He was, however, on the CIA watch list. Probably on the FBI list, too."

Which meant that RJ Katz and David Dillard might also be acquainted with him. It was entirely possible that every person staying at the safehouse knew Maser—a circumstance that irritated Paul. Each of these people had looked him in the eye and denied knowledge of John Maser.

He glanced toward Julia. Did she know? Was this another lie she'd told him?

Leaning forward in his chair, Paul matched Gil's aggressive posture. "Were you aware that Maser was in this area?"

"No."

"Did you kill him?"

"Hell, no."

"Why should I believe that? You already lied to me about knowing him."

"If I'd taken him out, it wouldn't be a sloppy kill. There'd be no details for you to investigate."

That was a scary assertion, especially since the second murder—that of General Harrison Naylor—had been completely free from damning evidence. "Are you an assassin?"

"Can't answer that question."

Another terse response. Trying to pull information from Gil wasn't easy. Paul leaned back in his chair. "Why the hell did you want to talk to me?"

"I meet problems head-on. You have suspicions about me. That's why you were in my bedroom." His gaze hardened. "You're wrong."

"Assuming I believe you," Paul said, unsure of whether or not he could trust a CIA assassin, "maybe you can help me."

"Sure. Why not?"

"Maybe if I tell you a little bit about this crime, you can give me a profile of the killer."

"Shoot."

"Maser's car went off the road at a fairly deserted spot. In regular circumstances, it might not have been found for days. But it happened that a tourist pulled off to take photographs and noticed the wreck. She flagged me down. I called it in."

"How do you know the accident didn't take place days ago?" Gil asked.

"Maser rented the car in Denver earlier in the day." Paul stared into Gil's fathomless eyes. "Maser wasn't there long. He was still alive when I climbed down the hill to offer aid."

"Did he say anything?"

"One word." *Murder.*

Paul allowed the pause to stretch between them. If Gil Bradley was nervous that Maser might have implicated him, he didn't show it. His posture was rock solid. It didn't even seem like he was breathing.

"He was covered in blood," Paul said. "His car flipped on the way down the hill, and he wasn't wearing a seat belt. He was banged up pretty bad."

Julia shifted in her chair, clearly uncomfortable with this description.

Gil said, "Sounds to me like nothing more than a car accident."

"That's the way it appeared," Paul said. "Even though there was no snow or ice on the night Maser went over the edge, these mountain roads are treacherous. The sheriff wasn't inclined to push the investigation until we found more evidence."

"Which was?" Gil asked.

It went against interrogation procedure to give information to a suspect. But Gil wasn't a regular suspect. Paul needed something to draw him in. "Usually, with this kind of car accident, we wouldn't bother with an autopsy. The Eagle County coroner would mark down cause of death due to external injuries and loss of blood. But it so happened that we were transporting the general for autopsy in Denver and Maser went along. Autopsy results showed Maser was drugged."

"Usually," Gil said, "you wouldn't have noticed."

"Whoever killed Maser was unlucky twice. For one thing, we found the wreck more quickly than we should have. For another, Maser's body had a detailed and expert analysis." He didn't take his eyes off Gil. "What can you tell me about the profile for this assassin?"

"It wasn't a professional job. A trained killer leaves nothing to chance." Gil's posture seemed to relax as he considered the murder. He steepled his fingers. "There's a cowardly aspect to this murder. The killer filled his victim full of drugs and sent him off a cliff."

"Why is that cowardly?"

"At the moment of dying, the killer didn't have to look his victim in the face. He didn't see the fear. The pain. The eyes bugged out in surprise. The gaping mouth."

Though Gil's voice was a low monotone, the picture he evoked was vivid. He'd been there. Paul knew, without doubt, that Gil had killed before.

And now? Was he an assassin for the CIA? Had he looked into the eyes of the general before he pulled the trigger?

"You know what it's like," Gil said. "You're a lawman, Paul. I'm sure you've seen your share of violent death."

Too often, he'd dealt with the victims of accidents or natural disasters. The crushed body of a cross-country skier caught in avalanche. The charred corpses of the fire-jumpers on Storm King Mountain. Hell, yes. He'd seen the aftermath of violence. But Paul had never killed another human being. He hoped with all his heart that it would never be necessary for him to do so.

Abruptly, Gil pushed back his chair and stood. "Good luck on your investigation, Deputy."

"I appreciate your cooperation."

In a few quick strides, Gil was at the library door. Over his shoulder, he said, "Even Johnny Maserati deserves justice."

"What did you say?"

"Johnny Maserati," Gil repeated. "That's what Maser used to call himself. Maserati. Like the fast car."

Paul had heard that name before. When he first mentioned John Maser, the general had referred to Maserati. General Naylor had known Maser well enough to use his nickname. These two murders were connected.

IN THE RELATIVE SAFETY of her bedroom, Julia locked the door and turned toward Paul. "Johnny Maserati. That's what the general called him. Right?"

"Right." He detached the holster from his belt and placed his handgun on the nightstand. Then, he sat on the edge of her bed to pull off his boots. "Did you know him, Julia?"

She couldn't believe he'd even ask that question. "Of course not."

"Maser was on the FBI watch list. I assume you have access to that information."

"I'm not a field agent. The watch list is nothing to me."

Without looking at her, he asked again. "You're sure you didn't know Maser?"

His doubts reminded her of her own deception and lies. After what she'd done, she probably deserved to be treated with suspicion. But she didn't like it.

She came around the bed to stand in front of him, planted her fists on her hips and waited until he looked up. It was important to her that he understand what she was saying. "I'm telling the truth about Maser. There are no more lies between us, and there never will be again."

"What about your FBI buddies? RJ and David? They probably knew Maser."

"I can't answer for them."

With his boots off, he sat on her bed, leaning back against the pillows and the headboard. His extra-large body and long legs took up a lot of space. "I'm pretty damn sure that everybody else in this safehouse is lying to me. FBI. CIA. A senator. All your so-called guests have their own special little agendas to protect."

"What about Gil?" she asked. "He seemed to be straightforward in his responses."

"He didn't admit to much. And I didn't question him about the general's death—a murder in a locked room. That kind of complicated assassination seems like it's more in line with an expert kill. The kind of work Gil might be real proud of."

She had to agree. "You're seeing a link between the two murders. The general. And Johnny Maserati."

"Yeah. Maybe." He nodded slowly. His eyelids were beginning to droop. "I'm too tired to think any more tonight."

So was she. But there were issues that needed to be handled before she got into bed beside him. "We're still in danger. One of us should stay up and keep watch while the other sleeps."

Paul rose from the bed and went toward the locked door. With a shove, he pushed her dresser so the edge blocked the entrance. "Anybody trying to get in here will make enough noise to wake us. And nobody is coming through the window. Not in this blizzard."

If that was his idea of protection, she wasn't impressed. Obviously, she could have managed this precaution all by herself. She reminded him, "I'm supposed to take the three a.m. surveillance shift."

"I'll go with you." Paul stretched out flat on the bed. He was lying on top of the comforter. "Turn off the light and wake me when it's time."

The other important issue was sex. Julia wanted to clarify their relationship before she climbed into the bed beside him. Her gaze traveled the length of his body—from his thick black hair to his feet, which were almost off the end of the bed. Her attraction to him was undeniable, but she didn't intend to make love to a man who thought she was a liar.

Julia had never been the sort of woman who indulged in casual affairs. If she and Paul made love, it had to mean something. "We need to talk."

"Not now."

His eyelids closed. In contrast to her own lustful thoughts, he wasn't showing the least bit of sexual interest in her. No subtle winks. No dimpled smiles. Paul looked like he was ready for sleep. And nothing more. *Damn it.*

Didn't he like her? When they first met, he'd asked her out on a date. He'd kissed her in the parking lot outside the skating rink. Was that sexual magnetism gone? Dead?

Irritated, she turned off the overhead light. There was enough illumination from the window to find her way around her small room. Should she change into her nightie? Peering through the dark, she saw that Paul's eyes were closed. His breathing was slow and steady. In about two minutes, he'd be fast asleep. *Damn it!*

Opening the top drawer of her dresser, which was now halfway in front of the door, she took out her long, totally unsexy flannel nightgown. She pulled her sweater over her head and peeled off her jeans, which were still slightly damp from being outside in the snow. In her bra and panties, she glanced over her shoulder at the bed. Paul didn't move a muscle. This total disregard was not what she had anticipated. With an angry tug, she pulled her gown over her head.

It was probably for the best that he wasn't interested in sex tonight. They'd been through a lot today, and it was too soon to be intimate. *Damn it!*

To be sure, she was physically drawn to him—his broad shoulders, barrel-sized chest and long legs. More than that, she approved of his profession, his lifestyle, his family. He embodied many qualities she looked for in a mate.

If they'd had a chance to date and gradually develop their intimacy, having him in her bed would have been cause for champagne and celebration. Tonight, it was obvious that nothing was going to happen.

After setting her alarm for three—less than five hours from now—she slipped under the comforter. With this very big man in the bed, there was only a sliver of mattress left for her. She nudged against him, trying to make room.

And then, he surprised her.

He turned to his side. His arm draped across her waist, and he pulled her against him. They fit together like two large spoons. His breath tickled her ear as he whispered, "You're beautiful, Julia."

"You watched me undress."

"I'm tired," he said. "Not dead."

In the darkness, she felt a smile spread across her face. *He thought she was beautiful.* The attraction wasn't gone. She snuggled more firmly against him. Through the comforter that separated them, she felt his belt buckle pressing into her back. If she rolled over and faced him, she knew they would kiss.

"Your hair…" He exhaled a sigh. His voice sounded utterly exhausted. "It's like silk. Smells so clean."

"It's too curly," she said.

"It's perfect." He lifted his hand to stroke the back of her head. "You've got a bump back here."

"It's where I was hit by the barn door."

"Does it hurt?"

"A little."

"Should I kiss it and make it better?"

"I wish it was that easy."

If she gave him the slightest encouragement, she knew he'd respond with all the passion that had been building between them since the first moment they laid eyes on each other. His arm wrapped around her again. His hand lightly massaged her torso below her breasts. She placed her hand atop his and anchored him firmly.

Moments ago, when she'd thought he wasn't interested in her, she was confused and frustrated, even angry. Now, he'd put her doubts to rest. He wanted her, too.

Her womanly instincts urged her to become his lover. What was she waiting for? They were two consenting adults, spooning in a too-small bed. Why not make love?

Because the timing was wrong. He wasn't with her because of their relationship. His concern was to protect her from physical danger. And he still had residual anger about the way she'd deceived him. Before they made love, they needed to talk. And they were both too tired.

"We should sleep," she said.

"If that's what you want."

"I do."

I do not. She wanted ever so much more. All his kisses. All his caring. She longed to hear him tell her a thousand times that she was beautiful.

And yet, she decided to wait. Her relationship with Paul had the potential of becoming something precious, and she would treat their moments together with the utmost consideration.

"Thank you," she whispered, "for being here."

"Good night, Julia."

Though she wouldn't have believed it possible for them to fall asleep in each other's arms without having sex, his embrace was warm and comfortable. The sound of his steady breathing was a lullaby. She felt herself drifting gently into slumber.

Her dreams flowed in pastel images. Flowers opened to the sun. Pink and yellow butterflies fluttered on the breeze. She stood at the edge of a waterfall. The cascading torrents played a soothing rhythm. The shimmering droplets moistened her cheeks. When she reached into the water, it was warm and soft.

A claw thrust out from the waterfall and grabbed her outstretched arm. In an instant, the skies turned dark and threatening. She was being pulled into the waterfall. She couldn't breathe.

She was struggling to escape when her alarm clock sounded and she woke up.

The comforter no longer separated her from Paul. She was snuggled against him. Her head rested in the crook of his neck. Their long legs entwined. His large hand cupped her breast.

Her alarm clock continued to beep.

Struggling away from his embrace, she hit the alarm and sat up. A weary groan pushed through her lips. The back of her skull ached. She needed to go to the bathroom. She wanted more sleep. Hours and hours more sleep.

Behind her back, she heard Paul moving. "Come back here," he growled.

"I can't." She turned on the bedside lamp, hoping that the light would erase the memory of her dream. "I promised to take the three o'clock shift."

"Let the other guys do it. You're the boss."

Which was exactly why she had to fulfill her responsibilities. Though she doubted that Roger or Craig were anywhere near as tired as she was, Julia needed to start behaving like the senior agent in this safehouse. To step up. To take charge. "Gotta do it."

Grumbling, he roused himself. His movements were slow and lumbering. He reminded her of a big, old bear coming out of hibernation as he stumbled toward the dresser and pushed it back where it belonged.

When he reached for the doorknob, she said, "Wait. We need to be careful."

"I'm just going to pee."

She reached for her handgun. "I'll cover you."

"For a trip to the bathroom?"

"Can you think of a better time for an ambush?" She didn't need to remind him that there was a murderer locked inside the safehouse with them. A murderer who had probably taken two lives.

He stretched his shoulders and rolled his head from side to side before he turned toward her. The hint of a smile touched his lips. "Julia?"

"Yes, Paul."

"We need a bigger bed."

Chapter Eleven

In the kitchen, Paul leaned against the counter and watched as Julia made a fresh pot of coffee. In spite of the fact that it was three o'clock in the morning, she looked good—neatly dressed in jeans and a V-neck red sweater. Her thick brown hair was pulled back in a neat ponytail.

Last night, his fingers had tangled in those wild curls. He'd held her close and felt her heart beating against him. Her body was full, strong and supple. Her skin was smooth as satin. Warm satin.

As she filled a mug for herself and for him, she was humming.

"You're a morning person," he said accusingly. "One of those people who do the rise-and-shine routine."

"It's my wholesome Midwestern heritage.

I like getting an early start on the day, baking bread, keeping a clean house."

But she also carried a gun. "How did a wholesome girl like you decide to join the FBI?"

"My psychological profile says I'm a self-motivator with a highly developed sense of right and wrong."

"You like chasing down the bad guys?"

"Not so much," she admitted. "I was a field agent for a while, and it wasn't real satisfying. I like helping people, but there's no big thrill in slapping the cuffs on a bad guy."

"Why did you stay in?"

"I really like being in authority." She grinned. "That means bossy. So, come with me. Now."

He followed her down the narrow staircase to the basement of the safehouse. At first glance, this looked like any other semi-finished basement with furnace, storage and several well-stocked pantry shelves. There was a laundry area with washer, dryer and folding table. Nothing special.

Julia unlocked a plain wooden door and pushed it open.

He'd never been in this room before, and his first impression was of white. White walls. White desktops. White tile floor. This office space had several computers and a bank of monitors showing surveillance from the many hidden cameras.

Agent Craig Lennox looked up when they entered. Nervously, he glanced toward a computer screen across the room from where he was standing. Then, he threw up his hands. "You caught me."

Julia went directly to the screen. The picture showed David, RJ, Gil and the senator sitting around a table.

"What's this?" Julia demanded.

Craig dragged his hand through his sandy hair. His skinny shoulders hunched. If he hadn't been wearing a holster clipped to the belt of his khaki trousers, he might have passed for a high school computer nerd. "I was curious about the Homeland Security meetings, and I planted a camera in the room and recorded them."

"You were spying," Julia said.

"Yes, ma'am."

"You know that's a breach of security."

He stalked toward the computer monitor. "I'll erase this disk and remove the camera."

"Not so fast."

She glanced toward Paul, and he gave a

quick nod. It might be handy to know what went on in these meetings.

"I'm curious, too," she said to Craig. "Did you record this earlier today?"

"This afternoon. It's mostly arguing. But from what I could see of the computer simulation, it's brilliant." Craig visibly brightened. "David Dillard is some kind of genius. He's set up an interactive program, posing a terrorist situation. Each of the other participants has their own laptop, providing them with additional information not seen by the others."

He crossed the room and pointed to the image on the computer screen. "See. At this point, they were all punching information into their computers. Then they'll discuss the problem and come up with solutions, deciding how to set up a task force to deal with the terrorist simulation."

"Sounds like a computer game," Paul said.

"A really amazing computer game," Craig said. "David has time limits imposed. When the participants respond, the situation changes. For better or worse. Or another event might disrupt their discussion. I'd really like to discuss the programming with David."

"But you won't," Julia said. "At least, you won't tell him that you've been secretly recording the sessions."

"Should I disconnect the meeting room camera?"

"Not yet," she said. "I can justify this covert observation on the basis of security. But let's not share that information with the others. Understood?"

A loopy grin stretched the corners of his wide mouth. "Thanks, Julia."

"Get some sleep," she ordered. "It's still snowing, and we're going to be busy tomorrow with the snowblower and the plow."

When Craig left the room, Paul went to the bank of six monitors. "I know you've got more cameras than this."

"Dozens of cameras," she said. "And dozens of sequences we can run them in. We pretty much keep the interior cameras going all the time. Plus one in the front of the house and one in the rear."

"What if somebody approaches from across the meadow?"

"We have a motion-sensitive system for outdoors. If anybody touches the fence, the surveillance camera comes on and we get a warning light on this grid." She pointed to another computer with an electronic diagram of the property. "Most of the time, those cameras record charming wildlife videos of deer or squirrels crawling over the fence, but we still need to respond and check it out, then record the security breach in our log report."

"Sounds like a lot of work."

"It is," she agreed. "We usually keep the exterior system turned off."

Paul nodded. There was such a thing as too much surveillance. These computers and electronic equipment must have cost the FBI a small fortune.

She took a seat in front of the monitor bank and tapped in a code on the keyboard. "I wish this camera had been on when I was attacked."

The screen showed the interior of the barn where the horses appeared to be comfortably bedded down for the night. As Julia watched the monitor, she smiled.

"You love those horses," he said.

"If I get reassigned and have to leave the safehouse, I'm really going to miss them." There was a softness in her blue eyes. "I love just about everything about the mountains."

"Even the weather?" He pointed to an outdoor camera at the front of the house that showed a steady snowfall. "It's really coming down. We've probably already got ten inches. The roads are going to be hell tomorrow."

"On the plus side," she said, "I don't think we need to worry about that guy who came after us at the skating rink showing up here."

The downside was that they were snowed in with a very clever murderer.

On the indoor surveillance monitors, he watched Craig's progress as he left the kitchen, went through the lower level, then up the staircase to the second floor and then to the third. Throughout the rest of the house, there was zero activity.

Paul took a sip of his coffee and glanced toward Julia. "What's your procedure? Is there anything special you do when on surveillance duty?"

"We'll walk through the house a couple of times at unscheduled intervals. And keep an eye on the monitors."

He glanced at the screens. Nothing had changed. Three hours of this was about as exciting as watching paint dry.

Crossing the room, he focused on the prerecorded session of the Homeland Security meeting. Nothing happening there, either. David, RJ and Gil were punching information into their individual computer keyboards. The senator leaned back in his chair, looking bored.

"Here's a thought," Julia said as she moved to one of the desks. "We can check out the FBI information on John Maser, also known as Johnny Maserati."

He stood at her shoulder and watched as her fingers dashed across the keyboard. The FBI logo flashed across the screen. "Is it legal for me to watch you do this?"

"Probably not recommended, but I'm not accessing any top-secret information. I imagine this is pretty much the same data you have in police files and the National Crime Information Center."

A mug shot of John Maser popped up on the screen. He was an average-looking guy, age forty-two. Quickly, Paul scanned his record. "Check his military history. Maser was a Marine. Let's see if he ever served under General Naylor."

Like all Marines, Maser was a marksman. He'd attained the rank of lance corporal before he was honorably discharged.

While Julia cross-referenced his postings with those of General Naylor, Paul wandered back over to the wall of monitors. Nothing had changed. Nothing had moved. The surveillance system provided a comprehensive look at the interior of the safehouse. How had a murderer gotten past this surveillance to enter the general's bedroom? "Is there any way of doctoring these tapes? Overriding the system?"

"Sure," Julia said. "But it didn't happen on the night the general was killed. Trust me, Paul. Nobody went through the door into his room."

"And he didn't share a bathroom?"

"Both the general and the senator have private bathrooms."

The murder was physically impossible. If that was true, why had Julia been attacked? Why had an assassin come after them at the skating rink? There had to be something they weren't seeing.

"Here." Julia pointed to the computer screen. "John Maser and the general served at the same time in the same place. They could have known each other."

"A lowly lance corporal and a general?"

"This was almost twenty years ago.

Naylor wasn't a general then. Only a lieutenant."

"Let's assume they were buddies." It was a starting point. "Maser could have been coming here to meet with the general. Why?"

"To warn him." Julia clicked off the FBI Web site and swiveled around in the desk chair to face him. "In Maser's gun deals, he might have come across information that indicated the general was in danger."

"Why would he care? According to our records, Johnny Maserati was little more than a fraud and a petty criminal."

"He was a Marine," she said as though that explained everything. "During that one period in his life, he behaved honorably and served his country. If the general was in danger, it was Maser's duty to warn him."

He remembered that her brother had been a Marine, and she had a lot of respect for the Corps. "Why wouldn't Maser warn the general with a phone call?"

She shrugged. "His message might have been too important to convey on the phone."

Paul understood that reasoning. Messages delivered in person were more effective. He took another sip of his coffee and rubbed his eyes. This was too much thinking. His brain hurt. He missed his usual seven hours of sleep. "Where does this logic lead us?"

Brightly, Julia replied, "Maser came to Colorado to warn the general that he was in danger. The killer intercepted him, drugged and watched as he drove off the side of a mountain. Then the killer carried out his original plan to murder the general."

Paul drained the rest of his coffee. "Now all we need is to ID the murderer."

Julia turned toward the screen where Craig's secret camera caught the four members of the Homeland Security team in action. "One of them. We'll know more after you interview them tomorrow."

"If they choose to cooperate."

He didn't expect these interviews to be easy.

AFTER THEY COMPLETED their surveillance shift, Paul and Julia went back upstairs and got ready to face the day. After his shower, Paul was still wearing yesterday's clothes. But he'd borrowed a razor from Craig and felt fairly clean when he left Julia's bedroom.

As he descended the staircase, he smelled breakfast—bacon, coffee and freshly baked muffins.

The others were already eating. RJ and David sat on one side of the long table. The senator and Gil were on the opposite side. Julia presided at the head. When Paul entered, she indicated an open seat beside David Dillard. "Please join us, Deputy. We were discussing the weather."

"Still snowing," David said. "The whole area is socked in. Airports are closed. The chain law is in effect over the passes."

"It happens," Paul said as he took a seat and immediately helped himself to pancakes and crisp bacon. Until this moment, he hadn't realized how hungry he was.

"I hate being confined," said RJ Katz. Her small hands busily sliced her food into tiny pieces. "This session has been a disaster. First, the general commits suicide. Then, we're snowed in."

In a sadistically cheerful voice, Paul said, "Don't forget the murder of John Maser, also known as Johnny Maserati."

The only one who showed any reaction to the alias was David Dillard. "Hey, I know something about Johnny Maserati. Isn't he involved with illegal weaponry?"

Ashbrook scowled at Paul. "I told you

last night that I refuse to answer any questions without a lawyer present."

"I heard you, Senator." Immediately, Paul looked away from the politician and gave his complete attention to David Dillard. "I appreciate your willingness to cooperate. You and me need to have a little talk after breakfast. Pass the syrup."

While Paul chatted about the food and potential for skiing after a blizzard and other mundane topics, he watched the senator out of the corner of his eye. Ashbrook dropped his fork loudly against the plate, sipped at his coffee and cleared his throat. His body language showed that he didn't like being ignored.

"David," Ashbrook snapped, "we should be getting started."

"Not for another half hour."

Pointedly, Paul said, "And David needs to talk with me. Shouldn't take long."

Again, he turned away from the senator. Without the proper warrants and probable cause, Paul couldn't compel Ashbrook to talk to him, especially since the senator demanded a lawyer be present. Ashbrook would have to decide for himself that he'd rather cooperate than be left out of the loop.

With breakfast done, Paul escorted David down the hall to the library where he'd talked with Gil last night. Taking a seat at the wooden library table, David appeared calm. He removed his black frame eyeglasses, took out a hanky and cleaned the lenses before placing them back on his pug nose.

Though Paul was only a few years older than David, he had a paternal attitude toward the wide-eyed computer specialist. Unlike Gil, David seemed inexperienced and eager to please.

Paul folded his hands across his comfortably full belly and said, "Tell me about Johnny Maserati."

"I never actually met the guy, but I ran across his name when I was doing research to create one of these simulations. It's the one we're doing today, and it involves a survivalist group."

Paul remembered the Wyoming survivalists associated with Ashbrook. "The Lone Wolves."

"I'm surprised you've heard of them," David said. "From what I can tell, they aren't dangerous. Their primary objective is to avoid paying taxes."

"Maser was supplying them with weapons."

"Possibly." David leaned across the table. "I don't like to point fingers, but Ashbrook has been involved with the Lone Wolves."

"How so?"

"Campaign financing."

David's information neatly validated facts that Paul already knew. "Is there anything else you recall about Johnny Maserati?"

"Not really. The only reason I recalled the name was because of the car. Maserati."

"Anything about his record when he was in the Marines?"

"Sorry," David said.

"Were you in the military?"

"My brother was a Marine. But not me. I went to college, got a degree in computer science and worked in Silicon Valley before I got recruited into the FBI."

"Recruited?"

"The gaming software I was developing had applications the FBI thought might be useful. When they contacted me, I jumped at the chance to get my hands on all the high end government technology."

They were getting off the subject. If Paul wasn't careful, he'd end up getting a lecture on megabytes and RAM. He brought the focus back to his inquiry. "How well did you know the general?"

Behind his glasses, David's eyes darted. "We met only a few times before this weekend. I still can't believe he committed suicide."

"Why is that?"

"General Naylor had a giant ego. It was more than self-confidence. He didn't think it was possible for him to make a mistake—surely not a big enough mistake to justify killing himself."

Though Paul hadn't known the general well enough to form his own opinions, he wasn't surprised by David's analysis. General Naylor had the reputation of being a leader of men. "Strong ego is probably a good trait for a general."

"Yeah? Tell that to Custer's troops."

"Sounds like you know something about the general's record. Can you give me some examples of his giant ego?"

"It's all in his book."

"I wasn't aware that he'd published a book."

"Every lamebrain pundit on television has a book deal," David said bitterly. "The general's book isn't in print. Not yet, anyway. He said that he planned to work on his manuscript while we were here."

Paul mentally reviewed the items he'd removed from the general's bedroom: clothing, the usual toiletries, a vitamin supplement, sleeping pills, three hardbacks including one on war strategy, a case for the general's hearing aid, a photo of his grandchildren. He hadn't found manuscript pages—nothing resembling the rough draft of a memoir. There had been, however, a laptop that was used to print out the general's suicide note. The manuscript must have been stored in the computer, which was now in the custody of the sheriff's department.

"I won't keep you much longer," he said to David. "Tell me when you arrived in the area and came to the safehouse."

"I came here the night before the exercises were supposed to start."

The night John Maser was killed. "What time?"

"It was after nine. I spent the day in Vail where I tried snowboarding."

"Did you like it?"

"Not much," he admitted. "I'm a whole lot better at computer sports than the real thing."

"After the snowboarding?"

"I had dinner and came here."

"Were you with anyone?"

He pushed his glasses up on his nose. "Sorry, Deputy. I haven't got an alibi until I arrived at the safehouse around nine or ten."

"Were any of the others here?"

"I don't know," David said. "I went directly to bed."

"Tired from the snowboarding?"

"Wiped out."

Paul recalled something Julia had mentioned. David suffered from insomnia. "So you didn't need a sleeping pill."

His eyebrows arched above his glasses. "How did you know about that?"

"It's my job to know. Did you take a pill?"

"I don't exactly remember."

David leaned back in his chair, withdrawing from the conversation. There was a wariness in his expression. Until now, he'd been cool and steady, even though he had no alibi. What was it about those sleeping pills?

Chapter Twelve

After her "guests" were back in session, Julia pulled on her boots, gloves and parka. Though Roger had already been out to the barn, she wanted to check on the horses. Stormy, the pregnant mare with the bad temper, wasn't expected to deliver for a week or so, but Julia was still concerned.

This marked the first time she'd been back to the barn since the attack, and she was glad that Paul had decided to come with her. Not that she was afraid to return to the barn. A well-trained federal agent didn't give in to fear. But she was definitely uneasy. Apprehensive.

Being confined in the safehouse with these four angry people—one of whom was likely a murderer—amplified her tension. Every word they spoke seemed to have a double meaning. Every gesture appeared threatening. Julia desperately wanted this impossible crime to be solved.

And when it was? She'd try to scrape together the shreds of her career and convince her superiors that she was still capable of running the safehouse.

"Ready?" Paul asked.

"Let's do it."

She shoved open the front door, and they stepped onto the covered porch. The storm raged before them. High drifts reached up to the porch railing. Though Craig had been out here with the snowblower clearing a path to the barn, the mounting snow had almost wiped away his efforts. It was white and cold.

"It's beautiful," she said.

"If you're a polar bear."

"I love when it snows like this. Unstoppable and fierce."

In comparison to the storm of tension inside the safehouse, the snow was wonderful and natural and clean.

She went down the steps from the porch and spread her arms wide, allowing herself to feel the full force of the storm. The heavy wet flakes pelted her cheeks and clung to her. If she stood like this for five minutes, she'd be covered in snow, turned into Frosty the Snow-woman.

Out here, there were no subtle motives. No secret ploys. The cold was real and exhilarating. When she laughed, puffs of vapor escaped her lips.

Paul tromped down the stairs. His shoulders hunched against the storm. "You're not going to flop down on the ground and make a snow angel, are you?"

"I might." But she had a better idea. Bending, she picked up a handful of snow and packed it into a ball.

"Don't throw that," Paul warned.

"Or else?" She shaped the ball with her gloves. "What are you going to do?"

"Lady, I will have to take you down. I happen to be the king of snow fights. Born and bred in the mountains, and I—"

She lobbed her snowball into his chest. "You're a nice, big target."

"Shouldn't have done that." In his huge hands, the making of a snowball took two seconds. He fired, hitting her on the shoulder. Before she could react, he pitched another one.

"You missed." Stumbling, she plowed through the drifts toward the end of the house. The wind pushed her forward. Scooping up another handful of snow, she packed it, turned and fired.

Paul retaliated with a direct hit on her shoulder. But she'd gotten a head start on him and easily escaped his next missile.

Behind the house, she ran as best she could through the knee-deep snow, stopping at the chopping block, which was almost buried. When she paused to make another snowball, Paul was right on top of her. Stumbling through the heavy snow, he caught up and wrapped his arms around her.

"What are you doing?" she demanded.

"You can't throw snowballs if you can't use your arms."

She struggled halfheartedly. In this moment, her mind was blissfully free from worry. She looked up into his handsome ruddy face. "Think you're so tough?"

"I know I am."

"Tough guys don't have dimples when they smile."

"Are you making fun of me?" His dimples deepened. "Now, you're in real trouble."

When he caught her under the knees and lifted her off her feet, she couldn't have been more surprised. Julia was a big woman.

Carrying her through a blizzard wasn't easy. She dropped her snowball and wrapped her arms around his neck. "Don't drop me."

Staggering, he headed toward a huge drift.

"I mean it, Paul. Don't you dare—"

When he tried to plop her down in the snow, she hung on tight and pulled him down with her. They were both wallowing in the snow. The hood of her parka fell back. Her hair was wet.

She should have been freezing cold. But when his lips claimed hers, an amazing heat flowed through her. This kiss had been building inside her for a long time—since last night when they lay together and throughout yesterday when she admitted she'd lied and saw anger in his dark, brown eyes.

Despite the raging blizzard, she was hot. A furnace flamed inside her. Apparently, all she needed to protect her from the elements was his kiss.

When he separated from her, she saw the reflected warmth in his chocolate-brown eyes. He wanted her as much as she wanted him.

He pulled her to her feet and glanced over his shoulder to the house. "Do you suppose we gave them a show?"

"Do you care?"

"Not really."

When they entered the relative warmth of the barn, she stamped her feet and brushed off snow. It was quiet in here. And peaceful.

And she was incredibly wet. Melted snow trickled down the back of her neck. When she unzipped her parka and pulled it off, a shower of snow fell to the barn floor. Rolling around in a blizzard hadn't been the smartest thing she'd ever done, but it was worth it. She'd gotten the kiss she'd been waiting for.

She saw Paul glance toward the corner where he knew a camera was placed. "Do you suppose the surveillance is operational?"

"It is." After her attack, she'd given instructions to run the barn camera 24/7. "But there aren't any microphones. We can talk freely out here."

"That's what I was hoping for."

Actually, she'd been *hoping* for more kisses. She was disappointed when he took out his cell phone. "Who are you calling?"

"First, the kids. Then, the sheriff."

"Did you get new information when you talked to David?"

"A book," he said. "According to David, the general planned to work on his memoirs while he was here this week. Since we didn't find any manuscript pages in his bedroom, he must have had it stored on his laptop."

"A memoir," she said. "The story of his life."

"Let's hope this book can tell us the story of his death. Who he loved. Who he hated. Who might have a good reason to want him dead."

Leaving Paul to make his phone calls, Julia went to Stormy's stall. Her gaze went to the far corner where she'd been left to be trampled in the hay. The mare paced nervously, pawing at the floor.

"Hush, Stormy. It's okay."

The horse whinnied. She reared up and came down hard. If those heavy hooves had connected with Julia while she was unconscious, she could have been killed.

Nonetheless, this was an inefficient murder method. She couldn't imagine Gil Bradley doing anything so haphazard. When he set out to perform an assassination, nothing was left to chance. Or was it? Maybe he'd claimed to be a cold-blooded killing machine to throw them off. Maybe Gil Bradley had lost his nerve. He'd been anxious to talk to them, and he made a point about looking into the eyes of your adversary at the moment of death.

In Gil's view, hitting her on the back of the head and dragging her body into a dangerous situation was cowardly. Similar to the way John Maser was killed. A supposed accident. There was little doubt that the same person was responsible for both assaults. The same murderer. And then, they'd hired a hit man.

Stormy calmed. She sidled up to the edge of the stall. Her big brown eyes seemed almost apologetic as she waited for Julia to stroke her nose.

"It's okay," Julia murmured. She took a piece of apple from the pocket of her parka and held it out. "I know you didn't mean to hurt me."

Stormy nuzzled her hand as she ate the apple.

"Being pregnant can't be much fun. Not that I'd know."

While Paul talked on the phone, she puttered in the barn, straightening the tack, checking the heating system, talking to the horses. There weren't any real chores to handle. Roger and Craig had done a good job out here.

Paul sat on a bench near the door, and she came across the barn to stand before him. "How are the kids?"

"They don't miss me at all. They're having a great time with Mac and Abby."

She was immensely glad his family hadn't been touched by the danger that surrounded the safehouse. "How much have you told Mac about the murders?"

"As little as possible."

"And how does he feel about babysitting?"

"He's trying to be cynical, telling me that I owe him big time for getting snowed in with the girls. But he's having fun. I can hear it in his voice."

"He and Abby make a good pair."

"Yeah, I'm expecting wedding bells real soon."

From the bench, he gazed up at her, and she saw the tension behind his easygoing expression. Their problems weren't over. Not by a long shot. "What did the sheriff say?"

"Because of the blizzard, he hasn't yet

returned the general's personal effects, including the computer, to his family."

That sounded like good news, but Paul's smile faded. His dimples disappeared.

"What's wrong?" she asked.

"The sheriff isn't inclined toward more investigation on the general's murder. I asked him to send me the memoir on e-mail, and he refused. We won't have that memoir to use for clues."

She hated to give up that potential lead. "It's possible the general brought the manuscript with him."

"Did you see him with the pages?"

"No, but he was the first to arrive. Came a day early, in fact. And he spent a lot of time in his room."

"There was no manuscript in his room," Paul said.

"But there might have been one," she said. "If the killer managed to slip into the general's room without being seen, it would be easy to steal away with the manuscript."

"In which case, we'll never find it," he pointed out.

"Not necessarily. Keep in mind that nobody but me has left the safehouse since the general's death."

"What are you saying?"

"We need to make a search of the bedrooms to see if we can find that manuscript." She pushed up the sleeve of her sweater to check her wristwatch. "They'll be in session for another hour before they break for lunch."

Paul was on his feet, ready to go. Though she'd wished they could spend a bit more private time together in the barn, the room search took top priority.

There were no snowball fights or kisses on their way back to the house. Now they had a mission. Search the rooms.

Inside the front door, Julia discarded her wet clothing quickly. In stocking feet, she padded toward the kitchen. Roger leaned over the stove, putting the last spicy flourishes on a huge pot of chili.

"Hey," she said, "good job with the horses."

"Is Stormy okay?"

"She'll be fine." She inhaled the spicy aroma. "That smells fantastic."

"The key is in the peppers," he said. "I made two versions. One with no meat."

Paul entered the kitchen and went directly to the stove. "Can I taste?"

Roger held out a spoon. Paul tasted,

licked his lips and made a low, prolonged groan—a sound that Julia suspected was more appropriate for the bedroom than the kitchen. Wryly, she said, "You like chili."

"I like food." Paul proudly stroked his barrel chest. "Especially chili. This is excellent."

"I like it hotter," Roger said, "but I figured these people from back east wouldn't appreciate three-alarm chili."

Paul nodded. "Serve it with hot sauce on the side. What brand have you got?"

Roger flipped open a spice cabinet to show off a row of Tabasco and hot sauce. As Paul started picking up each small bottle and studying the contents, it was clear to Julia that he was enthralled with Roger's collection.

She cleared her throat. Time was running out before the morning session ended, and they needed to get their room search underway. "I'm going upstairs to change linens on the beds. Paul, would you like to help?"

"You bet." He dipped the spoon for another taste of chili. "Be with you in a sec."

She headed upstairs to get started. Changing bed sheets and towels was a good excuse to be in the rooms of her guests, but it wasn't her favorite chore, especially since the dirty linens would then need to be laundered. She started with RJ's bedroom.

After the bed was stripped, Julia carefully went through the dresser drawers and closet. RJ's clothing was simple and well cut. No frills. Her underwear drawer showed a different side to her personality. Thong-style panties. Skimpy bras in exotic colors. Under RJ's tightly wrapped exterior beat the heart of a sexy vamp.

Beside the desk, Julia found RJ's briefcase. It was large enough to hold a manuscript, but when she lifted the locked case, it wasn't heavy enough to hold a ream of paper. Julia ignored the many other computerized devices stored in the drawers of the desk. Her goal was to find a manuscript.

Her search proceeded quickly. Not under the bed. Not between the box spring and mattress. Not behind the dresser or desk.

When Paul entered, she was already tucking the new sheets onto RJ's bed. "Nothing in here."

"How about the bathroom?"

"She and David share the bathroom. There aren't many hiding places. It's a plain, functional room."

He went through the bathroom door.

As soon as she smoothed the down comforter on top of the bed, Julia joined him. "Anything interesting?"

He was going through the contents of the mirrored medicine cabinet above the sink. "It's hard to tell who belongs to what. Everything is jumbled together."

"Let's assume the cosmetics are RJ's."

He shot her a grin. "It might be more fun if they weren't."

"Paul, we need to hurry."

"Apparently, both RJ and David suffer from insomnia. There are two different brands of sleeping pills."

"David mentioned that," she said. "RJ gave him one of her pills, and he didn't like the effect. It gave him bad dreams."

"The general took sleeping pills, too."

She suspected their high stress jobs were the cause of insomnia. Or ulcers. Or any number of nervous disorders. "I don't think it's all that unusual for these people to have trouble sleeping."

"There's an added significance," he said. "The autopsy tox screen on the general indicated that he'd taken two sleeping pills. They weren't his regular brand."

This really didn't seem like a big deal. These three people shared a common condition. Likely, they'd talked about their insomnia and swapped medications.

"It was this one." Paul held up an amber prescription bottle. "The general had taken two of these. The label says they belong to RJ."

"What's the dosage?" she asked.

"One or two per night. As needed."

An extra sleeping pill, especially in a different prescription, might have caused the general to sleep more soundly than usual. Still, it was hard for Julia to imagine him staying asleep while the murderer dressed him in his uniform and shoes. "Did the autopsy indicate an adverse reaction to the medication? Like a stroke? Or a coma?"

"No."

As she gathered up the used towels in the bathroom and replaced them with fresh ones, she repeated, "We need to hurry."

David's room was messier than RJ's. Yesterday's clothing draped carelessly over the back of the desk chair. The contents of his pockets, including breath mints and a couple of hankies, lay on top of the dresser. Like RJ, he had several electronic devices, including one that stored and played music. In his underwear drawer, she found a couple of condoms. She held one up for Paul to see. "Is it possible that David and RJ are having a fling?"

"I don't get that impression."

She carefully replaced the condoms in the exact place she'd found them. "Maybe David is indulging in a little wishful thinking."

They finished up in his room and went to Senator Marcus Ashbook's larger bedroom with the private bathroom. Despite the lack of a television, this was considered the luxury corner suite.

While Julia picked up the used towels and stripped the bed, Paul searched in the nooks and crannies. He paused at the window that overlooked the driveway leading up to the house. "Still snowing."

"Thanks for the weather report. Keep looking. We've only got a couple of minutes."

"Ashbrook has good taste," he said from inside the closet. "Nice clothes and shoes."

She carefully remade the queen-size bed.

The senator would surely complain if his covers weren't neatly tucked in.

Paul rummaged through the desk drawers. "Got it."

He held up several printed pages. The manuscript.

Julia rushed over to join him. Ashbrook had to have taken these pages from the general's room. This was more than a juicy piece of evidence. This was an indictment. Ashbrook had killed the general. She didn't know how or why. But she was certain that the honorable senator from Wyoming had somehow engineered General Naylor's suicide. Relief flooded through her.

She took a deep breath. Then she gasped as she read the title page. *"My Life in Politics* by Marcus Ashbrook."

"These are his own memoirs."

"Are you sure? Flip through the pages."

Paul scanned quickly. "Growing up on the ranch. His first vote on the floor. His work with Homeland Security."

Her short-lived satisfaction imploded and crumbled. "This isn't a clue. It's an ego trip."

Too bad. She really disliked Ashbrook. It would have pleased her immensely to place this murder at his doorstep.

Chapter Thirteen

After lunch and the afternoon chores were done, Julia and Paul went into the basement office where Craig was watching the Homeland Security session on his hidden camera.

Julia pulled up a desk chair to sit beside him. "You know we shouldn't be doing this. Spying on the spies."

"Should I turn it off?"

"No way," she said. "What's going on?"

"Today's computerized simulation deals with a bunch of survivalists. They're holed up in a compound in Wyoming and are refusing to come out."

"Similar to what happened in Waco." Julia shuddered, remembering the terrible consequences of that siege. "I'm kind of surprised. This isn't something I consider a terrorist issue."

"True," Paul said as he took a seat behind her. "I'm never quite sure what kind of situations fall under the jurisdiction of Homeland Security."

Craig pointed to the screen. "That's exactly the point they're debating. Jurisdiction."

"Turn up the volume," Julia said.

The three of them leaned forward to watch the real-time transmission from the room down the hall. In normal circumstances, Julia would never condone this covert observation. Not only was their unsanctioned camera a breach of the rules, but there was something creepy about spying. At the same time, it was fascinating. The picture on the computer monitor was like a made-for-television movie. They ought to be watching with a bowl of popcorn.

The petite RJ Katz came across very well on the screen. Her edgy hostility seemed almost attractive. Like a crusader, she was vehement in her insistence that a siege with an extremist group within the borders of the United States should be handled by the FBI.

Gil argued back that strategic groups within the CIA were better trained and equipped to infiltrate the perimeters of the survivalist compound and take control of the situation.

The senator sat quietly, biding his time. Like a poisonous spider, Julia thought, waiting to strike.

On the large screen behind the Homeland Security people, a well-defined graphic showed the outer walls of the computer-generated compound where the survivalists were under siege—several plain, clapboard buildings encircled by a high chain-link fence.

"We need more information," Gil said. He typed a command into the laptop in front of him. "I'm calling for aerial surveillance with heat-sensing capability to see how many people are inside and where they are."

Immediately, the computer graphic of the compound was replaced by an aerial photo.

"Wow," Paul said. "How was that done?"

"I told you," Craig said. "David is brilliant. Every probability is accounted for. They mention a strategy, and it's there."

Using his computer, Gil zoomed in on one sector. He squinted at the image on the screen. "That looks like a bomb. David, am I right?"

David Dillard stepped away from the

wall. "You're right, Gil. There is a bomb within the compound."

RJ typed on her keyboard. "I'm getting the data. Inventory of weapons. Warheads. Missiles."

"How can you do that?" Gil asked.

She gave him a smug look. "Follow the money."

"I don't get it."

"How many times do I have to tell you? This is my area of expertise. I can access inventory, bank accounts and transfers. All of it." She glanced up at David. "You've made it easier for me. Usually, this type of research would take hours."

They all watched as she typed, occasionally muttering to herself.

Her fingers leaped off the keys as though they had suddenly become red hot. "Oh my God!"

"What is it?" Gil demanded.

RJ's eyes were wide. She appeared to be genuinely alarmed, drawn into the computer simulation. "This bomb could be a nuke. We can't risk a violent takeover. They might detonate the device."

"We need immediate action," Gil said. "We send in my CIA team using extreme caution. The team will include a specialist to disarm the bomb."

As Julia watched, she was getting caught up in the drama of their simulated situation. Real lives were not at stake, but she felt the rising tension.

"Are you with me?" Gil asked.

"I don't think we should provoke them." RJ looked toward David, who was leaning against the wall, apart from the others. "As a technology expert, what would you suggest?"

"If the firing mechanism on the device is computerized, I might be able to jam it. But that's risky. I could just as well set it off."

"No good," RJ said. "What else?"

"Brainwashing techniques," he said. "We soften them up by bombarding the compound with audio messages, suggesting their surrender."

"What if they can't hear us?"

"That's a problem," David conceded. "We might find a way to introduce narcotics into their drinking water."

Gil scoffed. "How long would this brainwashing take?"

"It could be awhile," David said. "And I have to admit that these techniques aren't efficient with a large, diverse group."

"We go on the offensive," Gil said in a low, urgent tone. "There's no other way."

The senator rose to his feet. With a practiced gesture, he brushed the silver hair back from his forehead. "We need to talk with the people in that compound."

"Forget it," Gil said. "The United States government does not negotiate with terrorists."

"It's not a negotiation," Ashbrook said. "They've made no demands other than to be left alone on their own land."

"Which they refuse to pay taxes on," RJ said. "Not that tax evasion is important compared to the fact that they might be in possession of a nuclear weapon. They must be disarmed."

The senator signaled David with an imperious wave of his hand. "Show us the photograph of their leader."

David tapped a few computer keys, and the screen transformed to a picture of a rugged-looking character with stringy blond hair.

"He doesn't look very terrifying," Ashbrook said. "He's not a devil. Not a genius. He's just a man."

"Get to the point," RJ snapped. "What's your plan?"

Ashbrook stood beside the projected photograph of the leader. "My solution is political. Man to man. I walk up to the door of the compound and talk them into disarming."

"Without negotiating," Gil said firmly.

"I'll be reasonable but firm. These men aren't really terrorists. They're Americans. Just like a lot of other people I represent. I can talk sense into them."

RJ gave a decisive nod. She turned to David. "Let's follow Ashbrook's scenario. What's the outcome?"

"It depends." He circled the room and held the senator's chair. "Have a seat. You'll need to type in your dialogue with the leader."

While Ashbrook returned to his position behind the laptop, Craig explained what was happening to Julia and Paul. "These interface sessions are cool. The dialogue appears on the screen. I don't know how David comes up with the responses."

"Sure, you do." Julia stood and stretched. "When you were in training, you took classes in profiling and hostage negotiation."

Craig's thin face pulled into a scowl. "All that psychology stuff."

"I'm sure that's the data David will use. He can program typical responses in a high stakes conversation."

Both Craig and Paul seemed mesmerized by the screen, but she'd seen enough of this simulation to understand the most important factor. This wasn't about a simulated group of survivalists in Wyoming. The reality was the dynamic of the small group of people in the room down the hall. Their mission was to set up a first response advisory team. And Senator Marcus Ashbrook had taken control. He'd assumed the leadership position. He'd gotten what he wanted.

If the siege had been real and Ashbrook solved the problem—as he'd said, man to man—he'd be a hero. Wouldn't that be a fine launching pad for a presidential campaign?

She hated to think of Ashbrook in a position of power within Homeland Security. His motivations seemed to be entirely selfish. He wanted to be front and center, standing before dozens of television cameras and proposing his solutions.

Julia wished that Gil or RJ had put up more resistance to him. If the general were still alive, he wouldn't have relinquished his authority so easily. When he was killed, the balance in the group was thrown off, tilted in favor of Ashbrook.

Was that enough motive for Ashbrook to arrange the general's murder?

She glanced back toward Paul and Craig, who were both glued to the computer monitor.

"Ashbrook is good," Paul said. "He's making progress in convincing the leader."

"But he hasn't mentioned the bomb," Craig said. "That's the real concern."

Julia returned to stand behind them. "You know this is only a computer exercise, don't you?"

"It could happen," Paul said. "There are a lot of extremist groups and conspiracy theory people. Even here in Eagle County. We've got our share of wackos."

"If this was happening in Eagle County, would you want Ashbrook handling the negotiations?"

He pulled his gaze away from the screen and turned toward her. "I don't trust him."

"Nor do I," she said. "Let's leave Craig to keep an eye on the monitors."

Barely interested in their departure, Craig waved goodbye.

In the cozy living room, Julia flung herself into one of the matching rocking chairs in front of the fireplace. "Ashbrook is using this group to gain a position of power within Homeland Security. He's manipulating the others."

"You've got to admit," Paul said, "his solution of confronting the leader was a hell of a lot better than Gil's assault team or that mumbo-jumbo David was spouting."

"Mind control isn't so strange," she said. "True, it's hard to pull off with a group. But one-on-one, it can be very effective."

With a sigh, he sat in the rocking chair beside hers. It seemed almost too small to hold his large frame. "How do you know about this stuff?"

"FBI training," she said. "Forensic psychology is really interesting. The profiling. Interrogation techniques. If you punch the right emotional buttons, you can make a person do just about anything."

"Like hypnosis," he said.

"Kind of."

An excess of nervous energy coursed through her veins, and she rocked vigorously. Though it was too soon for her to be experiencing the effects of cabin fever, she felt trapped in this house. And frustrated by their lack of progress in solving the general's murder. If only they'd found the manuscript for his memoirs.

Pushing out of the chair, she paced to the front window and looked out. Though snow was still falling, the storm's fury had abated. "It's letting up."

"We're running out of time." Paul left his chair and joined her. "How much longer are these people going to be here?"

"Two more full days." Through the window, she saw Roger with the snowblower, clearing a path. "When we're not snowed in, you won't have a good reason to stay here."

"Protecting you." He eased up close behind her. Gently, his arms encircled her waist. "That's all the reason I need."

Leaning against his broad chest, she drew warmth and comfort from his nearness. Though he might want to stay with her, she knew it was impossible. Paul would be required to get back to his job. His children needed him. "There's no way I can justify keeping you here as a bodyguard. Not without explaining my suspicions. If I make that explanation, I'll have to confess that I tampered with the crime scene."

"Not necessarily." He nuzzled behind her thick curly ponytail to whisper in her ear. "We were threatened at the skating rink. If I tell the sheriff about that guy in the ski mask, he'll want me to stay with you."

And she wanted him to stay, wanted to keep him close. Tilting her head, she encouraged him to nibble at her ear. His breath was hot and moist against her throat. A shiver coursed through her—a shiver that had nothing to do with the cold. She longed for release. Sexual release.

Outside the window, Roger made another pass with the snowblower. "Nobody's watching," she said. "Craig is engrossed in his spying. He's not keeping an eye on the house monitors. Roger is outside."

"Then no one will see if I do this."

He spun her around in his arms and pulled her against him. Her arms stretched to wrap around his huge torso. She loved the way she fit against him, the way he held her close felt so good. So right.

"We shouldn't be doing this," she murmured. "I'm in charge of the safehouse. I should be setting an example."

His lips silenced her. With his kiss, he

exploded the apprehension that had been building inside her. Her defensive wall of propriety crumbled to dust. With a soft moan, she gave herself completely to this fierce, demanding passion.

Her mouth opened hungrily. His probing tongue thrust inside. She couldn't breathe. Didn't want to. She was overwhelmed. Blissfully overwhelmed.

When he separated from her, she gasped. Her heart beat throbbed like a big bass drum. It took a big man to sweep her off her feet. Paul was that man.

"Nobody's watching," he said.

His hand slid inside her sweater and cupped her breast. His thumb flicked across her taut nipple causing an electric thrill to chase through her.

"We should use this time to search."

As soon as the words left her lips, Julia couldn't believe she'd said them.

"What?" His eyebrows pulled into a frown.

"The manuscript."

"The general's memoir?"

"We can search the lower floor of the house. Nobody will question what we're doing."

His large hand gently squeezed her breast.

"That was the last thing on my mind. But you're right."

She didn't want to be right. She wanted him to kiss her again, to throw her down on the leather sofa, tear off her clothes and make love to her. "Damn it."

Paul kissed her forehead and stepped away from her. "Tonight," he promised.

"Yes. Tonight."

When she turned away from him, her legs wobbled as if she were intoxicated, drunk with passion. She blinked, forcing her eyes to focus. "Let's start in here."

They looked under chairs and behind shelves for the manuscript. While Paul checked the upper shelves in the hall closet, Julia stared into the fireplace where bright flames danced across her hand-split logs. "If I were the killer, I would have burned the manuscript."

"What would be the point? I'm sure there are other copies. Probably on the general's laptop."

"That could take months to surface." And they needed proof now. "Let's try the library."

It seemed like a very logical place to find a manuscript. Julia was familiar with the shelves and the books, which were half fiction and half reference books. Since the usual residents at the safehouse were protected witnesses involved in legal proceedings, there was a row of law books. At first glance, the library looked the same as always.

On shelf after shelf, she reached behind the rows of books and felt around, hoping her fingers would touch the loose pages of a manuscript. But there was nothing. Not on the shelves. Not inside the closed lower cabinet.

Paul stood beside the table where he'd sat to question David and Gil. The wood grain on the top was scratched and worn. In the middle was a drawer. He pulled it open. "Julia, come here."

Inside the drawer was a red pen and a stack of white paper. The page on top read: *Memoir of Harrison Naylor.*

"This doesn't seem like a hiding place," she said.

"Too obvious," Paul agreed

"He must have left it here."

Her mind formed a picture. She imagined the general sitting in the library with his red pen, editing his memoirs. She lifted the pages and flipped quickly through them. The first fifty were heavily marked in red. There was nothing after that.

"He stopped here," she said. "Chapter Six."

"It's like he was planning to come back to it," Paul remarked. "That doesn't sound like the action of a man who intended to commit suicide."

Carefully, she placed the pages on the table. Finally, they had a tangible piece of evidence. She could only hope that the general's written words about his life would be enough to spark a full investigation into his death.

Chapter Fourteen

In the kitchen, Paul helped Julia prepare dinner. Stuffed pork chops for the carnivores. Plain stuffing for the vegetarians. The side dishes included peas with pearl onions, buttered squash and a salad of romaine lettuce and artichoke hearts. Dessert was a chocolate cake. It was a simple but hearty meal. Comfort food to soothe the belly on a cold winter night.

Likewise, the next step in their investigation was uncomplicated. While everyone was gathered around the table for dinner, Paul would mention that they had located a copy of the general's life story. From the response, they might be able to figure out who knew about the memoir and who might be threatened by the general's remembrances.

It wasn't definitive evidence. No smoking gun. But they didn't have much else to go on.

Forensic evidence was nil, and the murder didn't even look like a murder. Their best hope was that one of their suspects would open up.

He telephoned his kids to see how they were doing and got a blow-by-blow report on the day's activity. The high point was when they caught Mac and Abby kissing. Then, Jennifer asked to talk with Julia.

Paul handed over the cell phone. He watched as Julia smiled and chatted, completely at ease while talking to a nine-year-old. Most people didn't know how to deal with kids. They either came across as stuffy advice-giving adults or they tried too hard to relate and acted like overgrown teenagers. Julia was perfectly natural—easygoing and pleasant with a great sense of humor.

Over the phone, she described their dinner preparations in detail. When she got off, she was smiling. "Don't be surprised when your daughter adds artichoke hearts to your next pizza."

"Why?"

"She thought it sounded gourmet. That's her word. Not mine."

"Swell," he muttered. "Were they complaining about my cooking?"

"Not at all. In fact, they said Abby is worse than you are. Apparently, she burned the microwave popcorn."

"The kids want to learn how to cook. And how to bake. And sew. And put on makeup." This refrain was familiar. And painful. "I can't teach them any of that stuff. I'm not, you know, a woman."

"Excuse me?" She bristled. "Are you saying housework is woman's work?"

"Hell, no." He'd stuck his foot in it this time. "I never got trained. My mom was traditional and never bothered showing us kids how she worked her magic."

Though Julia shot him a warning glare, she let the subject drop. "Where are your parents now?"

"They moved to Flagstaff about ten years ago. It was just after I got married, and I bought their house."

"The house where you're living now?"

"That very one."

It had been a sweet deal, requiring zero down payment. But Paul often wondered what his life might have been like if he hadn't been tied down so young with a house, a wife and kids. He loved the mountains. And he was well suited for his job as a deputy. But sometimes, he wondered what might have been. "I haven't led a very adventurous life."

"Some people say that raising kids is the best adventure of all."

"You know what I mean. I haven't seen the world, haven't tried a lot of things."

"Like what?" she asked. "Do you have an urge to go parachuting? Bungee jumping?"

"I've done those two," he said. "Didn't much care for the bungee jump."

"Come over here and sit." She directed him to the kitchen table and placed two cooled layers of chocolate cake in front of him. "Would you please frost these and stick them together."

"I can do that."

Wryly, she added, "It doesn't exactly require the skills of a pastry chef."

Using a flat knife, he smeared a glop of frosting on the top of one layer. "My friend Jess is always telling me about exciting stuff. He spent one summer in Baja, lying in the sun and swimming with the whales."

"Is that something you'd like to do?"

"Maybe." But he wasn't much of a beach person. And he knew that any travel plans would have to include the kids. If they weren't with him, he'd miss them too much to enjoy himself. "What about you, Julia?"

"On my vacation last year, I worked in a rural community that had been destroyed by a tornado. Rebuilding the houses, repairing the water system and electric."

"Doesn't sound like much of a vacation." He carefully placed one layer of cake on top of the other.

"Sure it was." She stood over his shoulder. "Hauling cinder blocks is a better workout than I'd ever get in a spa. I met some fantastic people. And I had the great satisfaction of seeing a completed project. A couple of brand-new houses for people who needed them. Fresh water pouring out of a faucet. It was a good adventure."

He tilted his head and looked up at her. "Hauling cinder blocks? Repairing plumbing?"

"That's right." She raised an eyebrow. "That's what I call women's work."

She was one hell of a fine woman. Too good to be true. When she talked about disaster relief work, it sounded like something he wanted to do. "Where have you been all my life?"

"Down the road twelve miles from Redding."

She reached around him, dipped a finger into the frosting and popped it into her mouth. Though he was sure she didn't intend for that gesture to be sexy, his eyes were drawn to her rose-colored lips. Slowly, his gaze traveled south. Over her shoulders. Down to the swell of her full breasts under her sweater.

Tonight, he reminded himself, they would be alone in her bedroom. Tonight, he would unfasten her wild, curly hair. He'd yank that ridiculous flannel nightgown off. Tonight, they would make love.

When she dipped again into the frosting, he objected, "Hey, save some for the cake."

She gave him a wink and started carrying dishes into the dining room.

It didn't take long for the troops to gather. Even Roger and Craig joined them at the long table. The mood tonight seemed more positive than before, partly due to the fact that the snow had finally stopped. According to the forecasters, they could expect sunshine tomorrow.

The attitude among the Homeland Security people was different. Almost friendly. Gil and RJ teased David about how they had out-smarted his simulation and averted disaster. The senator basked in his leadership role, and Paul had to admit that Ashbrook wore that status with dignity. He was gracious, steady and concerned. It seemed that a pecking order had finally been established in this group. Ashbrook was on top.

Paul waited until the cake was served to drop his bombshell. "Julia and I happened to find an interesting document today."

"Tell us about it," Ashbrook said.

"A memoir." He watched for their reaction. "General Harrison Naylor's memoir."

"I knew he was working on it," David Dillard said.

Gil and the senator commented on how the general's life story was especially important in light of his recent passing. They lifted their glasses in a toast.

RJ remained silent.

"I WISH RJ had spoken up." Julia flopped crosswise on the bed in her room. "There was something on her mind. That's for sure."

Paul closed and locked her bedroom door behind himself. Tonight, he wanted to be sure there would be no interruptions. He placed the general's memoir on top of her dresser. "RJ had her opportunity to come forward. I asked her again if she'd sit down for a talk, and she turned me down."

"What's she hiding?"

"The answer might be in here." He tapped the top sheet of the manuscript. "RJ was the only one who seemed worried that we'd found the memoir."

"The only one who *showed* concern," Julia corrected him. "I guess we should start reading."

"In a minute."

"Did you have something else in mind?"

She turned to her side, bent her elbow and propped up her head. Her sweater outlined the womanly curve of her waist and the fullness of her hips.

Though Paul was plenty tired after being trapped inside the house all day, her hour-glass figure enticed him. The promise of tonight was the only thing that had kept him going through another long day. He stretched out on his belly beside her. The bedsprings creaked under their combined weight.

Paul shifted himself around, trying to find a comfortable position. No matter which way he turned, his feet dangled off the edge of the mattress. He rolled onto his back. "At my house, there's a king-size bed."

She snuggled up close. "There are certain advantages to a small bed."

"Like cold feet that stick out from under the covers?"

"Like this," she whispered.

Her long legs straddled his hips as she climbed on top of him. The weight of her breasts pressed against his chest. Her action surprised him, but he was glad she made this move. Very glad.

"Wait," he said. "Unfasten your ponytail."

She tore off the barrette and her thick hair cascaded around her shoulders. He glided his fingers through the silky length. Reflected glow from the overhead light shimmered in the vibrant curls.

Her lovely face loomed above him. If she wore any makeup, he couldn't tell. Her complexion was fresh, clean, beautiful. Her blue eyes darkened with a sensual promise meant only for him.

When they kissed, he was immediately aroused. He'd been waiting all day for this. Maybe longer. Maybe he'd been waiting all his life for Julia.

There was a knock at the bedroom door.

"Not now," he grumbled.

Another knock. He heard RJ's voice. "Excuse me? Deputy Hemmings?"

He wrapped his arms more tightly around Julia. "Maybe if we ignore her, she'll go away."

"You know we can't do that." She dropped a kiss on his cheek and climbed off him.

Oh, man! Paul squeezed his eyes shut, willing his frustration to go away. Every cell in his body wanted to make love to Julia. Why was this so impossible? He liked her. She liked him. If there was any justice in the world, they should be lying together naked.

Instead, there was RJ. She'd picked the worst moment to intrude.

Julia opened the door and confronted her. "What is it, RJ?"

"I'm ready." Her mouth drew into a prissy little bow. "I've decided to answer questions from Deputy Hemmings."

He couldn't say no. But he sure as hell wasn't going to invite her into the only privacy he had with Julia. Paul grabbed the memoirs from Julia's dresser and tucked them under his arm. No way would he leave this evidence unprotected. "Let's all go down to the library."

By the time they entered that familiar room, Paul's patience was at an end. He sat across from RJ and fired off questions to determine her whereabouts during the time frame when John Maser crashed his vehicle. RJ had no alibi. None of these people did. That would be too easy.

Paul charged into his next line of inquiry with all the subtlety of a bull elephant. "You were upset when I said we'd found the general's memoir. Why?"

One of her small hands rubbed across her mouth, and her gesture reinforced his first impression that she was like a cat. She might be preparing to lick her fingers and groom herself.

Her small hands folded neatly on top of the table. "I wasn't on friendly terms with General Naylor."

"Something in the past?"

She nodded and lowered her head, staring down at her own hands. It was obvious that she was having trouble getting the words out, but Paul wasn't in the mood for gently leading her toward a confession. "You wanted to talk to me, RJ. What do you want to say?"

"It's a long story."

Julia sat beside her and placed her hand atop RJ's. "It might be easier if you started at the beginning. How did you first meet the general?"

"At Arlington Cemetery."

"At a funeral?" Julia prompted.

"Four funerals. There were four Marines killed in the line of duty because Naylor had made a stupid mistake in judgment. A failure in leadership."

"Did you know these men?"

"No." She raised her head. Her hazel eyes widened as she looked at Julia. "I was there with my former fiancé. A Marine sergeant. The men being buried were his friends. He'd been injured in the same incident. He lost his left arm below the elbow."

"I'm sorry." Julia felt RJ's small hands trembling. Her skin was icy cold. "What was your fiancé's name?"

"Garret. He shouldn't have been out of the hospital, but he insisted. He needed to be with his men."

Julia understood her former fiancé's

motives. Her brother had been the same way. "The Marines put duty first."

"And Garret loved being a Marine. It was his whole life. With his injury, he knew that he'd never be cleared for active duty. He was devastated."

Julia nodded. Though RJ wasn't her favorite person, she sympathized with her tragedy. Someone she loved had suffered a terrible loss. "Was General Naylor any help?"

"Not one damned bit." Her tone was as furious as the harsh winds that rattled the windowpanes. "When I met him at Arlington, he gave me the standard 'sorry for your loss' speech. And he told Garret to pull himself together. As if he could. As if he could grow another arm."

She pulled her hands away from Julia's grasp and folded her arms below her breasts. A tremor rocked her shoulders as she continued, "Naylor was an insensitive bastard, and I told him so. Right there in Arlington in front of those long rows of white crosses, in front of everybody. I never thought our paths would cross again."

"But they did?"

"Several times. The general never returned

to the field. For the past couple of years, he has been focused on Homeland Security, which is also my area. Whenever I could, I made it my business to put General Naylor in difficult situations."

"Like this weekend?"

Her eyes glittered with suppressed hostility. "I was looking forward to these simulations. I wanted to show Naylor what an incompetent fool he was." She turned toward Paul and repeated those words with careful enunciation. "Incompetent. Fool."

"Got it," Paul said.

"But not likely to commit suicide," RJ said. "That's why you're really here, isn't it? You think Naylor was murdered."

"Is that why you were concerned about the memoir?" Paul asked.

"He might have mentioned me. Something derogatory. To tell the truth, I'm not sorry Naylor's dead. But I didn't kill him."

Julia waited for this angry outburst to settle. It bothered her that she hadn't picked up on this feud between RJ and the general. When she'd seen them together, they hadn't acted like sworn enemies. Paul asked, "Did you know John Maser, also known as Johnny Maserati?"

"No."

He fired off another question. "RJ, do you have insomnia?"

A puzzled look crossed her face. "I do."

"You're not the only one."

"David's worse than I am," she said. "He's always so wired that he can't sleep."

Julia asked, "Do you and David share information about insomnia?"

"Sure. We even swap pills."

"What about the general," Paul asked. "Did you give him some of your sleeping pills?"

"No," she said coldly.

"Why not? He also had trouble getting to sleep."

"Too bad for him. There's no way I'd help him. If he was drowning, I wouldn't throw him a rope." Her eyes narrowed and she glared at both of them. "But I wouldn't shove him overboard. I'm not a murderer."

She most certainly had motive. Julia couldn't remember the last time she'd seen such venomous hatred. "You never finished telling us what happened between you and Garret."

"After he lost his arm, he was a changed man. The psychologists said he suffered from survivor's guilt and posttraumatic stress. Depression. I pleaded with him to get help. To learn to use his prosthesis. But he wouldn't do anything." Her spine stiffened. "Garret never really recovered. He quit the Marines. And he quit our relationship, too. He kept pushing me away until I finally gave up."

"You don't stay in touch?"

"The last I heard, he was living on disability. Hardly ever leaving his apartment." She shrugged. "If you want more information, you'll have to ask David."

"How does David fit into this picture?"

"Garret is David Dillard's brother."

Chapter Fifteen

Instead of one motivated killer, they had two. Both RJ and David might blame General Naylor for what had happened to Garret.

After RJ left the library, Julia closed the door behind her. She should have known about this connection, should have asked more questions. David had mentioned his brother in the Marines. He and RJ were friendly enough that they volunteered to be in the rooms that shared a bath. "If I had talked to them, I could have gotten this information a lot sooner."

"Don't blame yourself." Paul glanced toward an upper shelf in the library where they both knew a surveillance camera was situated. "Is there audio surveillance in this room?"

"A bug?"

He nodded.

"Not usually." But she was well aware of Craig's secret audio and video in the meeting room. And the safehouse was occupied by other agents—Gil, David and RJ—who were capable of planting their own listening devices. "If you'd like, I could do a sweep and find out if anyone is listening."

"I'd appreciate that," he said. "Seems to me that we should stay down here and start reading these memoirs."

A twinge of disappointment went through her. "Instead of in my bedroom?"

"I think we both know what will happen if we go to your bedroom."

She knew. They'd make love. The inevitability of their passion was an awesome force, constantly surging through her. She wanted him. But she also wanted to solve this crime, and there wasn't much time left. These suspects would check out of the safehouse in two days. As soon as the blizzard stopped, Paul would be gone.

Glancing over her shoulder at the almost-invisible lens of the surveillance camera, she reined in her natural urges. Paul was right. The general's memoir was a clue they couldn't ignore. They should stay here. "You're right. We need to look at the memoir."

"I'd feel a lot better if I didn't have to worry about being recorded."

"I'll be right back."

She went down the hall and through the dining room to the basement staircase. In the office, she found Roger in front of the monitors. "Nice dinner," he said. "The cake was really good."

"Thanks. It's my mother's recipe."

He swiveled in the desk chair. "Julia, what's going on? I know Paul's here to investigate that car crash, but what does that have to do with the general's suicide?"

"I hope there's no connection." She opened a cabinet where electronic equipment was stored.

"Do you think the general killed himself because of that guy from the car accident? John Maser?"

"I don't know what to think."

"Me, neither. But I'll tell you this. I'm going to be real glad when these Homeland Security people are gone. They're too intense for me."

"Ditto." She found a handheld bug

sweeper and closed the cabinet. "I'll take the three a.m. shift again."

"Fine with me. I'll leave a note for Craig."

As she hurried back to the library, it occurred to her that Roger and Craig should also be considered among their suspects. She didn't really know much about either of these young agents. They might have reason to hate the general. Buried secrets.

In the library, she found Paul hunched over the table, reading the manuscript pages. "Anything interesting?"

"This is about the early years. His sainted mother and stern father who was a lawyer."

Quickly and efficiently, she swept the room and found no evidence of a listening device. "We're clear. What did you want to talk about?"

"The sleeping pills." He leaned back in his chair with his long legs stretched out in front of him. "RJ swears she didn't give the general her pills. But the autopsy showed he had taken a couple of pills with that formula."

"RJ could be lying."

"Why? It's not like the sleeping pills were poison or anything."

Julia remembered a conversation about

insomnia. "David said he had a bad reaction when he tried RJ's pills. Bad dream. Paranoia."

"Unreasonable fear," Paul said. "That pretty much describes the way the general was acting the first time I met him."

"When he was shooting rabbits off the deck." That incident seemed like a hundred years ago. "He said something about the media."

"He thought they were after him," Paul said. "Paranoia."

"Maybe that's a side effect of the sleeping pills, but it still doesn't explain why RJ might have given them to the general. If she intended to kill him, wouldn't she want him to be unsuspecting?"

"Good point." He straightened the pages of the manuscript. "Maybe another side effect is really deep sleep. So the general wouldn't wake up when somebody came into his room and shot him in the head."

"That doesn't explain why he was dressed in his uniform." Even though she knew the library was free from audio surveillance, she lowered her voice. "With his medals incorrectly displayed and his shoes unpolished."

"What happens to a Marine who isn't up to snuff?"

"A reprimand," she said. "Especially for a general. It would be humiliating."

"Whoever killed him might have done the medals wrong on purpose. To show that General Naylor didn't deserve to be a Marine."

"Whoever killed him." All of their investigation came back to the same thing. The murder was impossible. There was no evidence to indicate that anyone had entered the general's bedroom.

Paul divided the manuscript in two and held out a stack of pages toward her. "Dig in. We need to get lucky and find a clue."

She went to one of the comfortable chairs in the library, turned on the lamp beside it and sat. Her belt holster jabbed her in the back. She unclipped it and placed her handgun on the small side table beside the lamp. Settling into the recliner chair, she popped up the footrest, got comfortable and started to read. The chapter heading was: "My Silent Battle."

In these pages, the general described a battlefield explosion resulting in a head trauma that caused him to lose sixty percent of his hearing. His writing style was straightforward and almost completely devoid of emotion. He wrote about the hospital where he stayed but never mentioned his pain. Or his family. "Paul, was the general married?"

"At least once." He looked up from the pages. "He mentions getting married in his twenties and calls her the first wife."

"What about his next of kin? Who claimed the body?"

"A sister," he said. "That makes me think there isn't a current wife. And probably no children."

"His whole life was the military," she said.

Though the general had achieved a great deal and traveled the globe and had innumerable adventures, his life story didn't seem to be a happy one. She flipped through the pages, wondering if he'd written them himself or if this was an "as told to" memoir.

Julia's eyelids were drooping before she got to the end of the chapter. She leaned back in the comfortable recliner. It had been another long day. She needed a second wind. A burst of energy. Maybe if she rested her eyelids…

It seemed like only a few minutes later when she heard Paul gently calling her name, and Julia opened her eyes and saw him hovering over her. His huge hand rested on her shoulder. His dark brown eyes looked directly into hers. "Are you awake?"

"Just resting my eyes."

"It's almost three. Time for your surveillance shift."

That couldn't be. Her brain struggled toward consciousness. "I've been sleeping? How long? Four hours?"

"Just about." He leaned down and kissed the tip of her nose. "Has anybody ever told you that you're pretty when you first wake up."

"Pretty embarrassed," she said.

He stood, went to the library table and picked up the manuscript pages. "Let's go downstairs. I found some good stuff in the general's memoir, and I want to tell you about it."

"Good stuff?"

"Important pieces of evidence." He held up two fingers. "Two of them."

She hauled herself out of the recliner, stretched and yawned. "I feel guilty for not helping."

"No problem. I even caught a couple of hours sleep myself."

"How did you wake up without an alarm?"

"I'm a light sleeper."

Paul had always been able to fall asleep when he wanted and wake up on time. That skill came in handy when the kids were sick.

He hustled Julia through the kitchen where they grabbed hot coffee. Then they went to the basement level. He waited while she settled herself at one of the swivel chairs and did a routine check on the monitors, including a peek into the barn where the horses rested peacefully.

The information he had uncovered in the general's memoir wasn't enough to solve the murder, but it might be enough to push for further investigation. *Really good stuff.*

"Ready?" he asked.

"You're excited," she said. "Did the general outline the murder method and point a finger at the killer?"

"Not quite. But this might be enough to get you off the hook for tampering with evidence."

Her beautiful blue eyes flashed. "Tell me."

"Here's what the general says." Paul held up a manuscript page and started reading.

"'I never claimed to be infallible. I have made mistakes in my life and in my career. My deepest, most heartfelt regret came when—'"

"Wait," Julia said. "This sounds familiar."

"He goes on to talk about an error in strategy that caused the death of four Marines. That must have been the incident RJ was talking about."

Julia nodded so vigorously that her ponytail bounced. "I've heard this before."

"Not exactly." He handed her the page. "You've read it before. This was the general's suicide note."

As soon as Paul had seen those words, he recognized the context. They were printed on a plain sheet of paper, signed by General Harrison Naylor and left on the desk in the bedroom where he died.

One of the most important pieces of evidence in the investigation of a suicide was the note. When the general's note talked about regret and failure, it went a long way toward convincing the sheriff that his death was self-inflicted.

Shaking her head in disbelief, Julia

studied the page. "It was a page from his memoir."

"Anyone could have printed it."

"But he signed it," she said.

"I'm sure he's left a lot of signatures for someone to copy. When I turn this over to the sheriff, it'll be enough to reopen the investigation."

"Are you sure?"

"One hundred percent sure," he said confidently. "Here's how these things work in Eagle County. We aren't equipped to handle a complicated homicide. We don't have all the fancy equipment or handwriting analysts on the payroll. The sheriff will turn this over to the state investigators. Or to the FBI. Your own people can look into the general's death."

"Which means the true nature of the safehouse can still be kept a secret."

"This probably fake suicide note will be their reason to suspect homicide." He gave her a smile. "Nobody ever needs to know that you tampered with evidence."

She should have been cheering and dancing up and down. Instead, Julia looked worried. "It doesn't seem right. I ought to report my actions."

He came around the desk and took her

hand. "Let it go, Julia. There's such a thing as being too responsible. If you make a full report, you'll likely lose your job here."

"Very likely."

"That would be a damn shame. I'd hate to have you shipped out of town when I'm just getting to know you."

She squeezed his fingers. "I'd hate to leave."

"Besides, you told Jennifer that you'd teach her how to bake. You don't want to break that promise."

When she stood and wrapped her arms around his neck, Paul couldn't help thinking of the other unspoken promise between them. Their need to make love, fulfillment of the attraction they felt for each other.

She broke away from him. "What else did you find in the memoir? You said there were two things."

"The other one isn't so dramatic. The general is talking about the 'threat at home,' which he says is as important as the threat abroad. He mentions the Lone Wolves survivalist group and how Senator Ashbrook has been shielding them. It's a tirade against Ashbrook and all other politicians."

"Enough to give Ashbrook motive to kill the general?"

Her voice was hopeful. Clearly, if Julia had the chance to pick, she'd choose Ashbrook as the murderer.

"We could ask him," Paul said. "It's only a couple of hours until breakfast."

In a matter of hours, this could be over and done with. Paul would present his evidence to the sheriff, and the feds would take over. He and Julia could step back quietly. If they could make it through the next few hours, the threat to them would be gone.

Chapter Sixteen

After breakfast, Paul stepped onto the front porch to join Senator Ashbrook. Once before, they had met on the porch and talked about the Lone Wolves. Today, they were both drinking coffee. Both maintained an uneasy edge of hostility.

The view that spread before them was spectacular. It was the kind of morning that should have gladdened Paul's heart. The snow had stopped, and in its place was a magnificent blue sky. The sunlight glistened on mounds of crisp white snow. Perfect for skiing.

"Beautiful scenery," the senator said.

"It is."

"The weather report said we had twenty-six inches of new snow."

"I believe it." Paul should have felt better than he did. He and Julia had done their part in setting up a further investigation. They'd survived being snowed in with a killer. It was almost over. Still, he had a sense of foreboding. Even on this sunny day, a dark shadow seemed to hang over him like a shroud.

"What's on your mind, Deputy?"

"Last night, Julia and I had a chance to read General Naylor's memoir. He didn't much like you, Senator Ashbrook."

"Lucky for me, he's not a voter in my state."

"The general made some harsh accusations about the way you handled the Lone Wolf situation. Said you were sympathetic to terrorists."

"Sympathetic?" he scoffed. "It's unfortunate that you didn't have a chance to see me in action during yesterday's simulation exercise. Believe me, Deputy, I know how to handle so-called terrorists."

"Tell me about it."

"Sorry. It's classified."

Not really. With Craig's hidden camera, Paul had seen plenty. "If those memoirs get published, it could damage your reputation. Did General Naylor tell you that he was going to mention you in his book?"

Ashbrook tried to look down his nose, but

he couldn't really manage the superior look because Paul was so much taller than he was. He settled for a sneering curl to his upper lip. "Let me explain something to you, Deputy. I'm a senator, a campaigner and, most of all, a politician. People take potshots at me all the time."

"That must tick you off."

"I've learned to deal with it."

"Do you ever want to take revenge?" Paul asked.

"I can't allow myself that luxury. I need to be circumspect and careful."

"I guess so." Like Julia, Paul didn't like the senator personally. He was condescending and manipulative. "I guess if politicians started murdering every person who said bad things about them, they'd all be serial killers. Enjoy your day, Senator."

Leaving his coffee mug on the porch, Paul went down the steps to the path leading toward the barn. Though he doubted that he could solve this impossible murder by himself, there was something in him that hated giving up.

In about an hour, around ten o'clock, he'd put in a call to the sheriff and tell him that the general had likely been murdered. And that murder was likely connected to the death of John Maser. He'd also have to explain about the FBI safehouse. That was going to make their conversation messy, but it was necessary for the sheriff to know what was going on.

At the same time, Julia would talk to her superiors. The feds would take over. Then he and Julia could sit back and watch the show.

Though it was all for the best to let the experts make the case, it didn't feel right to simply hand over their hard-won bits of evidence and conjecture to other investigators. Not until he knew the truth. It would have given him great satisfaction to take the murderer into custody.

Outside the barn, he met Julia coming out the door. She was dressed in snow gear from head to boot, but the hood of her parka was tossed back and wisps of curly hair bounced around her face. She tromped through the deep snow and directly into his arms. Though he held her tightly, an embrace through all these layers of clothing was like hugging a pillow.

"It's almost over," she said.

"You'll be safe. And I'll be heading for

home." He wanted to believe that, wanted to be certain that everything would turn out fine. "Will you miss me?"

"I hope we'll be seeing each other again."

"Count on it."

"It's kind of a shame," she said. "We've spent all this time together and haven't had much chance for fun. Are you up for an adventure before we make our phone calls?"

"That depends." He recognized the mischievous gleam in her blue eyes. "What have you got in mind?"

She led the way to the large garage beside the house. Though the snowdrifts piled high as the windows on the north side, she pushed open a double wide doorway. Inside, she lifted the covers off two gleaming snowmobiles. One was black. The other, metallic blue. "I've only had these out once this season."

"Let's make it twice."

He loved snowmobiling, especially on a day like today. It took only a minute to haul the machines outside, climb on board and point the runners toward the open field.

"Follow me." Julia started her engine.

Until they were a good distance away from the house, he followed her at a slow speed. In the snow-covered field, Paul revved his engine and let loose. He swooped across the open snow, spraying a wake of champagne powder.

At the edge of the forest, Julia followed a wide path into the snow-laden trees, climbing the hillside. The route was tricky; these weren't manicured ski slopes. But these snowmobiles were made for navigating through rugged terrain.

He wished the kids were with them. Lily was still too small to operate a snowmobile, but Jennifer could do this. She was a decent skier, though she preferred figure skating.

At the top of the hill, Julia waited for him. They were surrounded by conifer forest, snow-covered peaks and a pure blue sky. He glanced back over his shoulder. From this distance, the safehouse was tiny. A plume of smoke rose from the chimney.

He was glad to be far away from the tension that had been building while they were snowed in. But he couldn't quite shake the feeling that the danger wasn't over. Not yet.

"Do you see that cabin?" She pointed through the trees and across the hillside.

Throughout these mountains were a system of warming huts used by backpackers in the summer and cross-country skiers in winter. "I'm surprised to see a hut so close to civilization."

"The only habitation around here for ten miles is the safehouse. If you follow the regular trails, it's a long hike to this cabin." She grinned. Her cheeks were red with cold, and her eyes were as blue as the sky. "Race you to it."

"What do I get if I win?"

"Me."

She cranked up her engine and took off.

No way was he going to lose this race. Paul dodged around rocks and trees, taking the steep hill at a precarious angle. He nearly overbalanced but adjusted his weight and kept going.

He beat her to the cabin with five yards to spare. He parked the snowmobile, got off and raised both hands over his head. "The winner and new champ is Deputy Paul."

"Real gracious," she said wryly.

"And now, the winner claims his prize."

"A trip to Disneyland?"

"A trip to Julia." He plowed through the deep snow and pulled her off the snowmobile into his arms. In spite of the wet cold that penetrated his jeans, he kissed her hard.

"You're freezing," she said as she struggled out of his grasp. "I'm wearing my snow gear. But you've just got jeans."

"Take me inside," he murmured. "Warm me up."

"With pleasure."

It was a small, one-room cabin with two bunk beds, a table and a fireplace with the logs already arranged to start a fire.

Paul found matches in a moisture-proof container on the mantel. "Whoever stayed here last did a nice job of preparing for the next visitor. The fire is ready to go. It's nice and clean."

"It was me," she said. "I like to come here to get away."

It was obvious that she knew her way around the cabin. She quickly pulled the mattresses from the lower bunks and dragged them close to the fireplace.

While he nursed the flame, she arranged several blankets and comforters on top of the mattresses. "Take off your pants," she said.

"That's pretty direct."

"I'm not talking about sex, Paul. Your jeans are wet and cold. Take them off."

"You first."

"No problem."

She peeled off layer after layer of clothing. Boots. Parka. Snow pants. Sweater. Regular slacks. Wool socks. It was like watching a butterfly emerge from a cocoon.

Her straightforward gaze challenged him, and Paul started taking off his own clothes. It felt good to get the cold, wet denim away from his legs.

Stripped down to her thermal underwear, Julia dove under the blankets on the mattress near the fireplace. In two seconds, he was beside her.

They held each other for warmth, sharing the combined heat of their bodies and waiting for the warmth from the fireplace.

"We're finally alone," she said. "No one knows we're here."

"Not exactly." He snuggled her lush body against him. "The snowmobiles made a lot of noise when we left the safehouse. And we've got smoke coming out of the chimney at this cabin."

"We're safe," she said firmly.

In Julia's mind, the danger was over. Nobody was coming after them. She intended to claim the next hour with Paul for herself. This would be their time.

She kissed the deep dimples on each side of his mouth, then she kissed his lips. It was a long, slow kiss to warm them up, and it worked well. When she separated from him, heat flowed through her.

Together, they removed their last layer of clothing. His huge arms enveloped her naked body. His tree-trunk thighs wrapped around her. She had never been with a man as big as Paul. He was overwhelming.

Her breasts rubbed against the crisp black hair on his chest. The friction of their bodies was amazing and arousing. Her nipples peaked. A groan of pleasure escaped her lips.

She wanted to be on top. Exerting all her strength, she rolled him to his back and eased herself across his chest. All the while, she rained kisses upon him.

He cupped her breasts, and a shudder went through him.

"Beautiful," he growled.

His hands roved her body. His touch was strong and demanding. He squeezed her bottom and fitted her against his hips so she could feel his hard erection. He was big all over.

When he flipped her onto her back, she

let out a shout of surprise. "Hey, what are you doing?"

He teased her with a smile. "I'm claiming my prize."

"Do you think you can toss me around like a rag doll?"

"Yeah."

"Think again."

She shoved back. They rolled off the mattresses onto the hardwood floor. She should have been cold. The crackling fire hadn't yet warmed the small cabin. But her blood boiled; she had never been hotter in her life.

Paul lifted her from the floor. They were standing. His body pressed hard against hers. He kissed her with mind-numbing passion. Just as hard, she kissed him back.

Wild and abandoned, they staggered against each other, intoxicated with the enormous desire that had been building for days. Her need was voracious and fierce. He retreated, and she pursued. His back slammed against the log wall of the cabin.

She heard a thudding noise. "What was that?"

Paul turned away from her to peer through the window. "We knocked the snow off the eaves."

When she looked out, he captured her again. She faced the window. Her fingertips touched the icy glass. From behind, he pressed against her. He held her breasts.

She spun in his arms, gave herself completely to their embrace. His touch consumed her body, her world, her consciousness. She whispered, "Take me."

"I didn't hear you."

Louder, she said, "I want you."

"What was that?" he teased.

"Make love to me." She was shouting. "Now. Paul. Now."

Her feet left the floor as he scooped her up and carried her back toward the fireplace. Together, they sprawled on the mattresses. He tried to cover her with blankets, but she threw them off. Too hot. Too damn hot.

She yanked him down on top of her. The weight of his body aroused her. She clawed at his back.

He groped for his jeans.

"What are you doing?" she demanded.

"Condom."

"Don't need it." Though she hadn't made love in years, had never made love like this, she was on birth control pills to regulate her cycles. "I'm protected."

There was a moment of stillness as they gazed into each other's eyes. She was gasping for breath. Her heart crashed against her rib cage. She was smiling, happy. Amazingly, utterly happy. Julia knew she had found the man she was supposed to be with. She whispered, "I'm yours."

When he spread her thighs, she was moist and ready for him. He entered her with a slow, tantalizing penetration. Her back arched. She called out his name. Softly at first, then louder.

He thrust against her. And she rocked back, echoing his fierce rhythm. Goosebumps covered her naked flesh. She tingled all over. The combined heat of their passion ignited in an earth-shattering eruption. Fireworks exploded behind her eyelids. More skyrockets than the Fourth of July. It was beautiful. She exhaled a ragged sigh.

He collapsed on the mattress beside her, pulled up the blankets and lightly kissed her forehead.

There was no need for talking. She lay quietly beside him, allowing the shivering aftermath of their lovemaking to pleasure her.

Moments passed before she opened her eyes. He was gazing down at her.

"You're loud," he said. "I like that."

"So are you."

"I hope all our racket didn't start an avalanche."

She grinned into his big, handsome face. "An avalanche of lust."

"The best kind."

She couldn't imagine being apart from him ever again. But he'd be leaving the safehouse today, after the other investigators moved in. "I wish we could have solved these murders."

"So do I." He lay on his back and stared up at the low ceiling in the cabin. "Do you feel like talking?"

"Maybe."

"We should try to get our facts straight before I call the sheriff and you contact your boss."

"I'll listen. You start."

"We've got good motive for all our suspects. RJ and David blamed the general for what happened to David's brother, Garret. Ashbrook wanted the general out of the way for political reasons."

"And Gil?"

"A man like Gil doesn't need a reason to kill," he said. "He just needs an order."

Usually, after lovemaking, Julia was lethargic. But she felt strangely invigorated—not enough that she was ready to jump up and run a mile, but her mind was alert and sharp. "Somebody like Gil would know other assassins. Like the guy who came after us at the skating rink."

"Right," Paul said.

"How is the general's death connected to John Maser?"

"Maser or Maserati knew all these people. And they knew him. My guess is that he got wind of a scheme to kill the general and was coming here to warn him. After living most of his life as a criminal, Maser was doing the right thing, trying to rescue his commanding officer."

"Once a Marine, always a Marine." But this explanation was still too vague. "How did Maser know?"

"Supposedly, he was in contact with the Lone Wolves, and they have information."

"About what?"

"That's what a more in-depth investigating team would uncover. Let's just assume the Lone Wolves knew the general was in danger and they told Maser."

"That seems to point to Ashbrook."

Much as she'd like to pin the murder on the senator, Julia added, "Gil knew them, too. And David used them as a prototype for his simulation exercise."

Paul pushed himself to a sitting posture. "Our main problem is that we still don't know how the murder was committed. Nobody went into that room."

"The general must have pulled the trigger himself," Julia said. "It's the only way."

"But why? It's not like he was brainwashed or anything."

"Maybe he was drugged." She sat up beside him, proudly naked. "We know the general took RJ's sleeping pills because they turned up in the autopsy. Sleeping pills that David said made him paranoid."

"It's a long step from paranoid to suicide." Paul leaned over and kissed her cheek. "We should get back to the safehouse and turn this over to the big-shot investigators who can put all the pieces together."

"Do we have to? I'd rather stay in this cabin forever."

His dark eyes turned serious. "We have a future, Julia. You and me. This won't be the last time we're together."

"Is that a promise?"

"You bet."

Though it seemed a shame to put out the fire they'd started only moments ago, they took care of cleaning up the cabin, leaving it ready for the next wayfarers.

Outside in the pearly snow, Julia looked back at the cabin. Their wild lovemaking had dislodged the snow on one side of the sloping roof—a fact that gave her an unexplainable burst of pride. She and Paul were good together. Really good.

She threw her leg over her snowmobile and reached for the starter.

"Wait," Paul said. "Do you hear that?"

A mechanical whine sliced through the crisp, clean air. Another snowmobile was approaching.

She saw him coming through the trees. A man in a black ski mask. He stopped at the edge of the trees. He was a good fifty yards away from them.

As she watched, he reached over his shoulder, bringing forward the rifle that was slung across his back. He raised the barrel and aimed.

Chapter Seventeen

In an instant, Paul reacted. He drew his handgun. Before the man in the ski mask could position himself, Paul fired three shots. At this distance, his accuracy was unreliable. Still, his bullets were enough to make the man in the ski mask duck.

Paul climbed aboard his snowmobile. "Go, Julia. Back to the house. Fast as you can."

"I'm not leaving you." She'd already drawn her weapon.

"He's got a rifle," Paul said. "Better accuracy. Better range."

"Then we need to get closer."

She started her snowmobile and drove directly toward the assassin. What the hell did she think she was doing? He had no choice but to follow. Gun in hand, he leaned down behind the windshield and raced after

Julia, praying she wouldn't get shot. *Please don't let her be hurt.* If anything happened to her, he didn't think he could go on living.

Their would-be assassin retreated. Down the hillside, he dodged through tree trunks until he swooped into the wide open expanse of the valley. His black snowmobile swerved away from the safehouse and disappeared into the trees.

At the edge of the forest, Paul and Julia halted. He leaped off his snowmobile and charged through the snow toward her. "Don't ever do anything like that again. You could have been killed."

She stepped off her snowmobile to confront him. "I figured he wouldn't have time to aim."

"You took a risk."

"What was the alternative? To run? To present my back as a target?"

Her cheeks flushed bright red. Her jaw thrust out in a stubborn line. He loved her strength and her fire. But there was danger that came along with her headstrong attitude. "You scared me half to death."

"I didn't mean to."

He guided her over to the shelter of a thick tree trunk. They needed to make plans.

"This attack was a repeat of what happened at the rink. We made a show of force, and he ran. But this time, he's got superior fire-power. He can hide and wait to pick us off when we cross the meadow."

"We could stay in the trees," she suggested. "Use the forest for cover."

Paul wished he knew the caliber and make of the assassin's rifle. He might be capable of pinpoint accuracy. He might be taking aim right now. "You head back to the house on a back route. I'll keep him busy, won't let him follow."

"You'd stay here? Exchanging fire with a hit man who has a superior weapon and probably unlimited ammo?"

"Right."

"I won't let you take that risk." She held out her hand. "Give me your cell phone. I'll call Roger and Craig for backup."

"No good," he said. "If they come racing out here, they'll be in as much danger as we are."

A gunshot echoed through the thin, cold air. The bark of the tree trunk beside him splintered.

He pulled her down behind an outcropping of snow-covered granite. They were trapped. There was no way to escape without taking a risk.

"I saw him," Julia said. "He's hiding behind the rocks shaped like rabbit ears."

From there, Paul knew the sniper had a clear view of the entire meadow. "You mentioned staying in the trees. Is there a path?"

"The long way around," she said. "But I'm not sure that's the best option."

"It was your idea," he said.

"That was before he almost shot our heads off from nearly a hundred yards away. That rifle has a telescopic scope. A good one."

"Like the rifle we found in Gil's bedroom."

"That's not Gil," she said.

Paul agreed. "He'd never turn tail and run."

"The problem," she said, "is that our sniper doesn't have to be close to be deadly accurate."

He understood exactly what she was saying. As soon as they started their snowmobiles, the assassin would know they were on the move. And he would follow. When he got within range, he could pick his shot.

Julia had another idea. "We could abandon the snowmobiles and try to sneak through the trees on foot."

"Not in this deep snow. We can't move fast enough."

"What are we going to do?"

"We have an advantage," Paul said. "There are two of us. And only one of him."

A plan began to form in his mind, but he didn't want to use Julia as part of his strategy. He wanted her safe and protected, shielded from harm. Though she was a federal agent, trained to react in dangerous situations, she was also his woman.

"We need to move fast," she said. "We don't want to give him time to set up and take aim."

"We'll start out like we're trying an escape through the forest," he said. "He'll follow us."

She nodded. "And then?"

"After we find a vantage point—like the top of a hill—you peel off. I'll keep going. Our sniper is going to stop so he can take aim at me. That's when you shoot him."

"I ambush him?"

"Right."

"I hate this plan." Her blue eyes were troubled. "You'll be a target."

"Not if you don't miss."

"It makes more sense for me to be the one who keeps going. I know the trails up here."

"No way. I promised you a future."

"Without you?" Her gloved hands grasped his shoulders, and she stared deep into his eyes. "I don't want to think about the future if you're not part of it."

"That's crazy talk."

She shook him. "I mean it, Paul. Until you showed up, I didn't even know I was looking for a man. But here you are. Pure gold. You're the man I've been waiting for all my life."

"And you—" inside his chest, his heart expanded; it was their destiny to be together "—you're everything I want."

"I can't lose you," she said. "I can't."

He gave her a quick kiss. "Don't miss."

HUNCHED OVER her snowmobile, Julia set a course through the trees behind the cabin where they had made love for the first time. With any luck, it wouldn't be the last.

There were two big flaws in Paul's plan. The first and most obvious was the danger to him. The second lay with her. She'd never shot anyone before. Of course, she knew how to use her weapon. On three other occasions, when she was acting as backup, she had aimed her gun at the bad guys. But it had never been necessary to pull the trigger. She didn't even enjoy hunting.

She told herself to be fearless, to be strong. This was a matter of life or death. Paul's life. She had to be accurate. If she got a chance for a first shot, there probably wouldn't be time for another.

Too soon, they approached the area where she would make her stand. Julia knew these backwoods trails well; this was her backyard. Near the top of a hill—the best vantage point for the sniper—the trail widened into a one-lane road. This route was used by forest rangers and BLM trucks, but there would be no traffic today. Mounds of snow covered the rocks and clung to the overhanging branches of trees.

At the edge of the forest, she guided her snowmobile behind a huge boulder. Glancing over her shoulder, she saw the tracks from her snowmobile. If the sniper came this far, he'd know she pulled off the trail. There might as well be a big red arrow pointing to her location.

Paul raced ahead, then doubled back. He was laying down two tracks through the snow so it would look like she'd kept going straight.

As she scrambled up the hill behind the boulder, his words echoed in her brain. *Don't miss.*

She had only seconds to position herself. Frantically, she pulled out her handgun and removed her heavy gloves. The weapon was as cold as death in her bare fingers.

She heard the drone of Paul's snowmobile pulling away. At the same time, the other snowmobile approached.

At the top of the trail, the man in the ski mask appeared. He killed the motor and pulled off the goggles that covered his ski mask. The place he'd chosen to stop was almost exactly where she had expected.

Weapon in hand, she braced her arms on a waist-high boulder. *Take your time. Don't panic.*

Then the unexpected happened. The sniper spoke out loud. "I have a visual on one of the subjects. Should I take the shot?"

What was he doing? He reached up, touched his ear and said, "It's the deputy. The woman must be farther ahead."

The sniper was in communication with someone. Wearing an earpiece. She gasped as a sudden realization hit her. She knew how the general had been killed. The most damning clue had been right there in front of them.

"You got it," the sniper said as he whipped his rifle into position and braced the barrel with his left hand.

No more time to think. Julia fired her handgun.

The sniper yelped. His left arm flung wildly. She had to have hit his hand. He threw himself off the snowmobile.

She took another shot. And missed.

When he rose from behind his snowmobile, he had an automatic pistol in his gloved fist. He was steady, professional. If he was in pain, he didn't show it.

Julia shot first. A direct hit in the center of his chest.

He fell back.

Her pulse beat in triple time. Had she killed him? As she stood for a better look, she heard the approaching whine of Paul's snowmobile.

The sniper was back on his feet. Not dead. Though his left arm hung at an odd angle, he wasn't disabled. He had to be wearing a Kevlar vest under his parka.

He turned and aimed downhill. Though she couldn't see Paul's approach, she knew he was racing back to help her. He could be killed.

"No," she said through gritted teeth. "Hell, no."

Her hand was steady. She took three more shots.

The sniper got off a couple of shots, then he darted into the forest on the opposite side of the trail.

The sound of Paul's snowmobile died. For one terrible moment, there was silence. Had he been hit? A gust of sheer terror blew through her, and she was chilled to the bone.

Then she heard a loud bellow. "Julia! Where the hell are you?"

"Here! I'm back here!"

"Cover me."

He stepped into her field of vision. Her focus was on the trees where the sniper had disappeared. She watched for any sign of movement, any indication that he might attack again. The branches of a conifer trembled, dropping a load of heavy snow. Though Julia couldn't see the sniper, she fired a warning shot into the forest.

Paul approached the sniper's snowmobile. He stayed low, keeping an eye on the forest, holding his handgun at the ready. His surefooted progress through the heavy snow showed a lifetime of experience in the mountains. Not too fast. Not too slow.

Leaning down, he grabbed the sniper's rifle. Using the snowmobile for cover, he aimed into the trees, peering through the telescopic sight.

"Come out and throw down your weapon," he shouted.

His voice echoed into the pure blue sky above the frosted mountains. There was no reply.

"I know you're injured," Paul yelled.

She heard the crunching of snow and saw a tree limb far down the hillside waver. The sniper was retreating on foot.

Paul called to him again, "We'll get you medical assistance."

That wasn't going to happen. This guy was on the run.

She stumbled out from behind the boulders. Fighting her way through the drifted snow, she made her way to Paul's side. "He's gone."

He slung an arm around her shoulders. "You're okay, aren't you?"

"Fine. You?"

He pointed to the torn sleeve of his parka. "He came close."

"Too close."

Though Julia loved her work as a federal agent, she never wanted to go through anything like this again. If she lost her assignment at the safehouse, she intended to apply for a desk job.

Paul said, "I thought I told you not to miss."

"I didn't. First I got him in the arm. Then here." She pointed to the center of her chest. "A direct hit. He must be wearing Kevlar."

"Figures."

Though the sniper was probably a professional assassin, she was relieved that he wasn't dead. Even in the line of duty, she didn't want to be a killer. What was it Gil had said? To see the fear in their eyes. Their gaping mouths.

She shuddered. "What do we do next?"

"We could track him through the forest. He's probably leaving a trail of blood."

"He's still dangerous," she reminded him. "He might not have his fancy rifle, but he's got a handgun."

"You're right. We'll leave the tracking to

a posse. I'll notify the sheriff." He stood. "Let's get back to the safehouse."

"One thing first." She pulled the key out of the snowmobile and slipped it into her pocket. "Now he won't be able to follow us."

"Smart," he said. "And we'll take a different route back to the safehouse so we stay clear of him."

He was already headed back to his snowmobile before she could tell him that she'd figured out how the general was murdered. The crime was solved. She had the answer.

Her revelation would have to wait.

Chapter Eighteen

Paul had serious concerns about the escaped assassin. If he made it out of the back country on foot, he'd be desperate. He could try a carjacking. Innocent people could be hurt.

Outside the safehouse, Paul used his cell phone to alert the sheriff. His boss wasn't happy. In the aftermath of the blizzard, the sheriff's department was busy—stretched to the max with accident reports, helping people with stranded vehicles and dealing with dozens of other snow-related problems. The last thing they needed was an armed and dangerous fugitive on the loose.

By the time Paul disconnected the call, the sheriff had made it damned clear that he was in trouble up to his eyebrows. And Paul knew it would only get worse when he started talking about how the general's suicide was actually murder.

Standing beside Julia, he looked toward the safehouse. "I don't want to go back in there."

"I can't leave," she said. "It's my job."

No job was worth getting killed for. "Let's get the hell away from this place. We'll go to the sheriff, turn over our evidence and let somebody else take over."

"Not quite yet." She reached up and gently touched the side of his face, compelling him to look at her. "Do you remember when we were talking about how we wished that we had solved this case?"

Those moments weren't something he'd soon forget. Everything that had happened in that little log cabin was branded in his memory. Every touch. Every taste. The way she had called out his name. "We were naked. In front of the fireplace. We'd just finished making love."

She nodded. "You said you wanted the crime solved. It was important to you."

"I suppose I did."

"What if I told you I have the answer? That I know how the general was killed?"

"I'd say you were hallucinating."

She took his hand and gave a light tug. "I want to go inside, talk to these people, clear up a few details and make an arrest."

He balked. Investigating on their own had proved disastrous. They'd nearly been killed. "If you really have this figured out, we ought to turn the evidence over to the sheriff. For once, we should follow procedure."

"And let these people lawyer up? You said it yourself. As soon as they know they're officially under investigation, they'll find ways around it. I want this to be over." Her eyes shone with determination. "I want to wrap up this case in a neat little package with a bright red bow on top. Please, let's give this a try. Trust me."

In his experience, when anybody played the "trust me" card, it meant trouble. Still, he agreed to go along with her plan. Because—God help him—he did trust her. She was strong, brave and smart. Especially smart.

As soon as she entered the safehouse, Julia informed Roger and Craig that they were on high alert. The situation was dangerous. No one was to enter the safehouse. Then she led the way down the staircase into the basement and down the corridor.

Without knocking, she shoved open the door to the meeting room. There were no windows. Floor-to-ceiling shelves lined the wall nearest the door. There were framed black-and-white photographs on the wall.

As Paul followed, he had the sense that he was being drawn in the wake of a curly haired speedboat, churning through perilous waters.

The senator sat at the head of the conference table. Gil stood beside the large screen at the far end where a computer image showed a Navy carrier. David and RJ sat side by side at the table.

"Please don't get up," Julia said. "There are a few things we need to discuss about the deputy's investigation."

"How dare you interrupt!" Ashbrook bolted to his feet. "We're in the middle of a session."

"Murder is inconvenient," Julia said.

"I intend to file a complaint with your superiors, Julia. You were supposed to provide a quiet place for us to meet. Instead, we've been—"

"Sit down, Senator."

"You can't order me around."

Paul stepped forward. He was cold and wet. In no mood for the senator's prissy objections. "Yes, she can. And you're going to sit there and listen."

The senator's eyes narrowed as he assessed Paul's attitude. Apparently, he decided that Paul was serious because he returned to his seat and stared pointedly at his wristwatch. "We can spare a few minutes."

"First," Julia said, "I'd like Paul to summarize your connections to John Maser, the man who was killed in the car accident."

Though he wasn't sure exactly what she was doing, Paul was more than willing to vent his frustration. While dealing with these people, he'd been thwarted at every turn. "The first time I talked to you people, every single one of you lied."

"What do you mean?" RJ asked.

She knew damned well what he meant. "You all told me that you'd never heard of John Maser, alias Johnny Maserati. Then I come to find out that he was on the watch lists for the FBI and CIA. You knew him. You all knew him. Gil was the first one to come forward with the truth."

He glanced toward the former Navy SEAL. His arms hung loosely at his sides. His weight was balanced on the balls of his feet, ready for quick action. Gil sure as hell had the contacts to hire a hit man. Was he behind these murders?

"According to Gil," Paul said, "Johnny Maserati was a mercenary trying his hand at gunrunning. And that's where you come into the picture, Senator Ashbrook."

Ashbrook waved his hand dismissively. "If you're talking about my tenuous connection to the Lone Wolves, that's old news. Everybody knows about it."

"Especially David," Paul said. "He talked to the Lone Wolves when he was researching his simulation. And if David had information, he probably told RJ. These two are a lot closer than you might expect."

"What do you mean?" Gil asked.

"Not that it's any of your business," RJ snapped. "But I used to be engaged to David's brother."

Gil scoffed. "There was a man willing to marry you? Hard to believe."

Julia waded into the conversation. "If you don't mind, Deputy, I have a few things to add."

"Be my guest."

"RJ and David are not only close friends,

but they share a common ailment. Insomnia. Isn't that right, David?"

"Yes." His eyes flicked behind his glasses. His arms folded defensively across his chest, and he tilted back in his chair.

"Sometimes," Julia said, "you even share medications. I believe RJ let David try some of her sleeping pills."

"There's no law against that," RJ said.

"Do those pills have any side effects?"

RJ shrugged. "None that affect me."

"I believe David mentioned bad dreams and a sense of paranoia."

"When you first start on these pills," RJ said, "that might be a side effect. But it goes away."

"There was another person who suffered from insomnia," Julia said. "General Naylor."

At the mention of his name, Paul noticed a sharpening of attention as if everyone in the room gasped at the same time.

Julia continued, "We know that General Naylor took RJ's sleeping pills. They showed up in his autopsy. It's likely to assume he might have suffered a side effect. He might have been paranoid."

The senator spoke up. "I fail to see any connection between the unfortunate suicide of the general and the investigation into Johnny Maserati's death."

Julia glanced toward him, and Paul took over again. "There's a link. They were together in the Marines. In spite of what Maser became in his later life, there was a time when he served his country with honor. I suspect he cherished that memory. That was why he came here. He'd heard rumors, perhaps while he was dealing with the Lone Wolves. Maser knew the general was in danger."

Ashbrook slammed the flat of his hand against the tabletop. "Not the Lone Wolves, again. They're harmless. You're making too much of them."

"In a further investigation, we'll be talking to them. Exploring the connection between John Maser and each one of you."

It was Julia's turn again. "John Maser knew the general was in danger. Someone was planning to kill him."

"This is absurd," Ashbrook said.

"And irrelevant," Gil added in his low, dangerous voice. "It doesn't matter who wanted the general dead. There was no possible way to murder him."

"That was part of the plan. Using my safehouse as an alibi for murder." Her angry gaze swept the room. "The plan was for the general to die in a locked room with a surveillance camera watching."

"Still doesn't explain the method," Gil said.

"You heard the answer in your simulation of the Waco siege," she said.

RJ surged to her feet. "How do you know what we heard?"

"We have a camera in your meeting room." Julia pointed toward the shelves by the door. "Right up there."

Every single one of them voiced an objection. Their work was supposed to be confidential. They were very important people. Spying on them was a terrible offense.

Paul listened to their complaints for a minute before he spoke. "Settle down. We're talking about the murder of General Harrison Naylor. That's a whole lot more important than your computer games."

Disgruntled, they quieted.

Paul finally had an idea of what Julia was

talking about. He sure as hell hoped she had more than a theory.

"In that session," she said, "one of the solutions proposed was brainwashing. Mind control."

All eyes focused on David. He was the expert in that area. He gave a nervous laugh. "You can't be serious. Do you think somebody hypnotized the general?"

"Something like that," she said.

"It doesn't work like that. Mind-control techniques are complex and subtle. It takes a long time to work into a subject's subconscious."

"You know all about mind control, don't you? You've been working on the general for a long time. And when the fatal night came, you made sure that he'd taken the sleeping pills that made him even edgier than usual. What was the next part of your plan, David?"

"How did this get to be my plan?"

"I'm guessing what happened that night," Julia said. "First, you suggested that the general print out a page from his memoir to use as a suicide note. And to sign it."

"How would I know what was in his stupid memoir."

"You hacked into his computer."

Paul was impressed with her reasoning. It all made sense.

She continued, "You chose the page where the general expressed regret for a mistake in strategy. A mistake that cost your brother his arm and threw him into a depression."

David stood. His arms were straight at his sides. His fists clenched.

Julia approached him. She was tall enough to look him directly in the eye. "Then, you suggested to the general that he dress in his uniform."

"No."

"You even told him to put the medals in the wrong order. Because he didn't deserve to be a proper Marine."

"You're wrong."

"You told him to lie on the bed and put the gun to his head. You were always talking to him."

"She's wrong." He appealed to the others. "How could I do these things?"

"Even at night when he slept, you were filling his head with subliminal messages and suggestions." Julia put her hand to her ear. "Through his hearing aid. It was more than a hearing aid, wasn't it? That piece of plastic that the general always wore was a transmitter. You could talk to him through it."

Paul blinked. The first thing he had noticed when he looked at the general's lifeless body was that he was still wearing his hearing aid. David had been using that transmitter to literally get inside the general's head, sending him mind-control suggestions.

No wonder the general was paranoid. He'd been hearing voices. It had to have felt like he was losing his mind.

Julia pressed David harder. "When did you make the switch? Was it when you talked to the general about the simulations? Maybe you even gave him a sneak preview. Put headphones on him and had him take out his hearing aid."

"No."

"Then you substituted the transmitter. It won't be hard to prove. The general's personal effects are still in the custody of the sheriff."

David took a backward step. Though

Julia hadn't touched him, he reacted as though he'd been slapped. He held up his hands, warding off her words. "I didn't shoot him. I didn't pull the trigger."

"You slowly, methodically poisoned his mind."

"He deserved it. He cost good men their lives. His mistakes were heinous. I'm right. Aren't I, RJ?"

Her eyes were wide. "Oh, David. What have you done?"

"The general ruined my brother's life. I couldn't let him get away with it. He had to pay." He backed himself into a corner. "The old man killed himself. If he hadn't already felt guilty, he wouldn't have been susceptible to mind control."

Paul took the handcuffs from his back pocket. "David Dillard, you're under arrest for—"

"Listen to me," David said desperately. "I didn't pull the trigger. He committed suicide."

"Maybe so," Paul said. "John Maser's death was more clear-cut. He was shot full of morphine."

"I didn't do that. You'll never prove that I did."

"We'll find something in the car," Paul said. "Now that we know where to look. We'll find fibers. A hair. Fingerprints. Something."

"Search all you want. It wasn't me."

There was the sound of gunfire from upstairs. The assassin! Paul tossed the cuffs to Gil. "Take care of this."

"With pleasure."

Paul dodged into the corridor and ran. Julia was ahead of him. She was almost to the staircase.

A man dressed in black crashed down the stairs into her. She lost her footing and fell back, sprawled on the basement floor. The assassin stood over her and aimed his weapon at the center of her chest.

Paul's heart stopped. He couldn't get off a shot fast enough to save Julia. Desperately, he shouted, "Wait!"

The assassin looked toward him. The left arm of his parka where Julia had shot him hung limp. The sleeve was empty but not bloodstained. A one-armed man. He could only be Garret Dillard.

Paul could see the resemblance to David in his brother's face, but Garret's eyes were sunken, filled with an abysmal depth of misery. In his short life, he had seen too much. He had experienced combat, loss and too much pain.

In a low voice, Paul said, "Put down the gun, Garret."

"Why?"

"So I don't have to shoot you."

"I'm ready to die."

He limped a few steps away from Julia but kept his handgun trained on her. Silently, Paul cursed her unthinking bravery. He loved this woman. He wanted to spend his life with her. His life. Not death.

"Naylor's dead," Garret said. "He got what was coming to him."

"And Johnny Maserati?"

"That little snitch," Garret scoffed. "Running to tell the general what he'd heard. I gave him a chance."

"You filled him full of morphine," Paul said, "and sent him down a mountain road."

"He could have made it. I've learned how to operate a vehicle while I'm taking morphine."

Easing closer, Paul tried to gage his shot. He didn't trust his marksmanship enough to aim at the gun. And Garret was wearing a Kevlar vest. It had to be a head shot. From the corner of his eye he saw Roger sneaking down the staircase.

"You don't want to shoot her," Paul said. "Her family has suffered enough. Her brother was a Marine, killed in action."

Garret focused on Julia. "Is that true?"

She nodded.

"Here's the deal," Garret said. "My baby brother didn't do anything wrong. It was me. All me."

Paul doubted that was true. David had the expertise to hack into the general's computer and to use mind-control techniques. That wasn't Garret. Not this pathetic shell of a former soldier.

"I understand," Paul said. "Put down the gun."

"You won't arrest my brother?"

"Not if he's innocent."

"Then we're cool."

As Garret raised the gun to his own head, Julia dove toward him. They crashed to the floor together. In an instant, Paul was on top of Garret, wrenching the gun from his hand. He flipped Garret to his belly and twisted his good arm behind his back.

Garret offered no resistance. He had surrendered.

Behind his back, Paul heard Julia talking to Roger, asking if he and Craig were all right. They were. Gunfire had been exchanged, but no one was injured.

Paul leaned close to Garret. "How'd you get here so fast?"

"Trained as a mechanic," he muttered. "Hot-wired the snowmobile."

"You're a smart guy," Paul said. "Both you and your brother."

It was a damned shame that they had allowed revenge to consume them. When General Naylor pulled the trigger, following David's instructions, he'd destroyed three lives. His own. David's. And Garret's.

THREE DAYS LATER, after the Homeland Security people were gone, Paul tromped along the pathway to the front door of the safehouse. Under his parka, he wore the black suit he usually kept for funerals and a striped necktie that his daughters said was classy. This evening, he was here for a date. A real date with Julia.

When she opened the door, he was momentarily taken by surprise. Of course, he knew she was beautiful. But he'd never seen her dressed up. Her hair was straightened, sleek and shining. She wore a soft blue sweater with a deep V-neckline. Her matching skirt fell just below her knees. On her feet were high boots that outlined her shapely calves.

He swallowed hard. "You clean up real good."

She gave a twirl, and her skirt flared enticingly. "I even put on makeup."

"Lean close. Let me see."

When she did, he gave her a light kiss.

She backed away. "Don't smudge my lipstick."

Julia had put in some serious grooming time for their date, and she didn't want to ruin the effect. Not until later. "Where are we going?" she asked.

"Jess suggested that I charter a plane and take you someplace spectacular."

"That sounds like Jess. How's he doing?"

"Yesterday, he skied for the first time this

season. Today, we moved him back to his condo in Vail." Paul grinned, and his dimples appeared. "He's going to ask Marcia—the nurse he's been dating—to move in with him. After spending all this time with my kids, Jess is ready to settle down."

"Just like Mac and Abby?"

Paul shrugged. "That leaves me as the fifth wheel."

"I guess that makes me the sixth wheel." Julia had some great news to share. "I'm not going to be reassigned, after all. Even though Ashbrook is still screaming for my head, RJ and Gil backed me up. I'll be staying here at the safehouse."

"Just twelve miles down the road from where I live."

When she took her coat from the front closet, he helped her into it, and he held the door like a gentleman. She wasn't accustomed to being treated like a lady, but it was something Julia decided she could get used to. "You still haven't told me where we're going."

"You'll see."

His first surprise was waiting outside. Instead of his Ford Explorer, there was a one-horse sleigh with a driver. In the back, they snuggled under warm blankets. In the cold December night, moonlight glistened on the snow, and the sky was filled with stars.

"I know you like the snow," he said.

"Love the snow."

With a jingle of sleigh bells, they lurched forward. When they turned onto a narrow path into the forest, Julia guessed where they were headed. "The warming hut."

"I wanted to take you somewhere secluded," he said. "So you could be as loud as you want."

As they neared the small log cabin, she saw the twinkle of lights strung along the eaves. "There's no electricity up here. How did you do that?"

"Generator. Mountain men are resourceful."

And that wasn't the end of his efforts. The interior of the cabin was something special. Light from the fireplace flickered on the log walls. There was a table set for two. Champagne. And, most marvelous of all, a king-size bed.

"All this for me?"

"I'd do anything for you, Julia."

"Promise?"

"You have my word." He took her into his arms. "And my heart."

She loved this mountain man. He was the man she'd been waiting for all her life, and she would never let him go.

HARLEQUIN®
INTRIGUE®

WE'LL LEAVE YOU BREATHLESS!

If you've been looking for thrilling tales of
contemporary passion and sensuous love stories
with taut, edge-of-the-seat suspense—then
you'll love Harlequin Intrigue!

Every month, you'll meet six new heroes
who are guaranteed to make your spine tingle
and your pulse pound. With them you'll enter
into the exciting world of Harlequin Intrigue—
where your life is on the line
and so is your heart!

THAT'S INTRIGUE—
ROMANTIC SUSPENSE
AT ITS BEST!

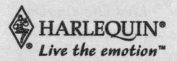

HARLEQUIN®
Live the emotion™

HARLEQUIN ROMANCE®

The rush of falling in love,

Cosmopolitan,
international settings,

Believable, feel-good stories
about today's women

The compelling thrill
of romantic excitement

It could happen to you!

EXPERIENCE
HARLEQUIN ROMANCE!

Available wherever Harlequin Books are sold.

HARLEQUIN®
Live the emotion™

www.eHarlequin.com

HARLEQUIN®
Presents

The world's bestselling romance series...
The series that brings you your favorite authors,
month after month:

Helen Bianchin...Emma Darcy
Lynne Graham...Penny Jordan
Miranda Lee...Sandra Marton
Anne Mather...Carole Mortimer
Susan Napier...Michelle Reid

and many more uniquely talented authors!

Wealthy, powerful, gorgeous men...
Women who have feelings just like your own...
The stories you love, set in exotic, glamorous locations...

Seduction and Passion Guaranteed!

HPDIR104

Harlequin Historicals®
Historical Romantic Adventure!

From rugged lawmen and valiant knights to defiant heiresses and spirited frontierswomen, Harlequin Historicals will capture your imagination with their dramatic scope, passion and adventure.

Harlequin Historicals . . . they're too good to miss!

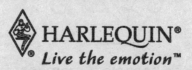

eHARLEQUIN.com

The Ultimate Destination for Women's Fiction

Visit eHarlequin.com's Bookstore today for today's most popular books at great prices.

- An extensive selection of romance books by top authors!
- Choose our convenient "bill me" option. No credit card required.
- New releases, Themed Collections and hard-to-find backlist.
- A sneak peek at upcoming books.
- Check out book excerpts, book summaries and Reader Recommendations from other members and post your own too.
- Find out what everybody's reading in Bestsellers.
- Save BIG with everyday discounts and exclusive online offers!
- Our Category Legend will help you select reading that's exactly right for you!
- Visit our Bargain Outlet often for huge savings and special offers!
- Sweepstakes offers. Enter for your chance to win special prizes, autographed books and more.

Your purchases are 100% guaranteed—so shop online at www.eHarlequin.com today!